I0773648

THE INVINCIBLES
TEAM ONE

BOOK FOUR

RILED

USA TODAY BESTSELLING AUTHOR

HEATHER SLADE

RILED

© 2020 Heather Slade

All rights reserved. No part of this book may be used or reproduced in any manner whatsoever without written permission, except in the case of brief quotations embodied in critical articles and reviews.

This book is a work of fiction. The names, characters, places and incidents are products of the writer's imagination or have been used fictitiously and are not to be construed as real. Any resemblance to persons, living or dead, actual events, locale or organizations is entirely coincidental.

Paperback:
979-8-88649-137-1

riled

/rild/

verb

to vex, inflame, provoke

MORE FROM AUTHOR HEATHER SLADE

BUTLER RANCH
Kade's Worth
Brodie's Promise
Maddox's Truce
Naughton's Secret
Mercer's Vow
Kade's Return
Butler Ranch Christmas

WICKED WINEMAKERS
FIRST LABEL
Brix's Bid
Ridge's Release
Press' Passion
Zin's Sins
Tryst's Temptation

WICKED WINEMAKERS
SECOND LABEL
Beau's Beloved
Coming Soon:
Cru's Crush
Bones' Bliss
Snapper's Seduction
Kick's Kiss

ROARING FORK RANCH
Coming Soon:
Roaring Fork Wrangler
Roaring Fork Roughstock
Roaring Fork Rockstar
Roaring Fork Rooker
Roaring Fork Bridger

THE ROYAL AGENTS
OF MI6
Make Me Shiver
Drive Me Wilder
Feel My Pinch
Chase My Shadow
Find My Angel

K19 SECURITY
SOLUTIONS TEAM ONE
Razor's Edge
Gunner's Redemption
Mistletoe's Magic
Mantis' Desire
Dutch's Salvation

K19 SECURITY
SOLUTIONS TEAM TWO
Striker's Choice
Monk's Fire
Halo's Oath
Tackle's Honor
Onyx's Awakening

K19 SHADOW OPERATIONS
TEAM ONE
Code Name: Ranger
Code Name: Diesel
Code Name: Wasp
Code Name: Cowboy
Code Name: Mayhem

K19 ALLIED INTELLIGENCE
TEAM ONE
Code Name: Ares
Code Name: Cayman
Code Name: Poseidon
Code Name: Zeppelin
Code Name: Magnet

K19 ALLIED INTELLIGENCE
TEAM TWO
Coming Soon:
Code Name: Puck
Code Name: Michelangelo
Code Name: Typhon
Code Name: Hornet
Code Name: Reaper

PROTECTORS
UNDERCOVER
Undercover Agent
Undercover Emissary
Coming Soon:
Undercover Savior
Undercover Infidel
Undercover Assassin

THE INVINCIBLES
TEAM ONE
Decked
Edged
Grinded
Riled
Smoked

THE INVINCIBLES
TEAM TWO
Bucked
Irished
Sainted
Hammered
Ripped

THE UNSTOPPABLES
TEAM ONE
Furied
Merried

COWBOYS OF
CRESTED BUTTE
A Cowboy Falls
A Cowboy's Dance
A Cowboy's Kiss
A Cowboy Stays
A Cowboy Wins

Table of Contents

Prologue

Rile

When I close my eyes, your voice floats through the jet's white noise and settles on my heart like a cold mist. And then you're gone. Always gone before I can make sense of the words you so desperately want me to hear. I stop short of crying out for you to say it again, beg like I always do, for you to stay with me and never leave.

I wait for the pain as it claws its way back into my soul. There's comfort in the familiar. At least I know I can feel…something. My eyes fill with unshed tears, and I murmur your name. *Celestina.* More than my northern star, you were my sun, my moon, my universe, my guiding light. Without you, I'm lost. So lost.

Forcing my eyes open, I look out the plane's window as we begin our descent to Mallorca, the island that has become my home because it's where you rest and will, for all eternity.

I stayed in my seat while the Bombardier taxied from the private runway to the hangar it shared with the much larger planes the DeLéons kept at their disposal. Part of me wished I could tell the pilot to turn around and take me back to Italy.

I stood, stretched my legs, and peered out another window when I saw my valet pull the black 1963 Mercedes-Benz 190 SL out of the same hangar the plane would soon be stored in. I smiled when he lowered the top; it was perfect convertible weather—sunny, but not too hot. May truly was the best month on the island.

I took one step down the plane's ramp when I was overcome by what felt like a hurricane-force gale, yet the air was still. I gripped the railing with one hand while I rubbed my temple with the other as the message came through, loud and clear.

Kensington is in danger.

1

"Thank you for agreeing to see me, Cortez," said the woman I'd known since I was a young boy and whom I still bowed to when in her presence.

"Of course, Your Majesty."

"Please be seated, Cortez. As you know, one of my husband's sisters has recently passed away, leaving her granddaughter somewhat at…odds. Do you know of whom I'm speaking?"

"Yes, ma'am."

"Kensington is a darling girl, but I fear her lack of parental guidance has resulted in her rather…irresponsible approach to life."

While I didn't know the details, I'd heard enough to wonder why the Queen didn't simply distance herself from the woman. The last I knew, Kensington had taken up with the great-great-great-grandson of the last of Austria-Hungary's monarchs, Emperor Karl I.

"I've received somewhat concerning news, Cortez," said the woman who was speaking to me now not as a former officer of MI6, but as my second cousin, once removed. "Given the delicacy of the situation, I've made the decision to keep the matter private rather than go to the prime minister."

"What's happened, ma'am?"

She looked over her shoulder as if anyone would've dared interrupt us and then leaned closer to me. "She's been kidnapped," she whispered.

"May I ask the source of this information?"

"I believe it's come by way of the girl's mother, my nephew's ex-wife, Kendra."

"May I also ask if she's been contacted by the kidnappers?"

"I'll leave those details to you, Cortez. I trust if anyone can locate her, it will be you." The Queen patted my hand and sat forward in her chair, signaling our conversation was over.

I stood, bowed, and left the same way I'd come in—through the family entrance. I was no sooner in my car than my mobile rang with a call from my mother. "Good afternoon, Duchess."

"How did your meeting go with the Queen, Cortez?"

"She believes Kensington Whitby has been kidnapped."

"You doubt it?"

I brushed my lower lip with my index finger, wondering how much my mother already knew. "My prediction is that it's more likely she's run off."

"What will you do?"

I smiled. The duchess knew exactly what I would do. "As requested by the Queen, I will handle the case as the kidnapping she believes it is. However, she has asked that the regular authorities not be involved."

"Your Invincibles will handle it, then, Cortez?"

I smiled. "Yes, Mother. Is there anything else you'd like to make me aware of at this time?"

"You know there's rumor of an involvement between Kensington and Konstantine von Habsburg?"

"I am."

"Perhaps, then, Budapest would be the place to begin your search."

"Anything else, Mother?"

"Be safe, Cort."

"I always am."

My prediction, while not an intuition, was that locating Kensington would be more of a nuisance than a mission. However, given the Queen was one of only two women alive I could never say no to, I would treat her grandniece's disappearance with the same level of tenacity and resourcefulness as any case I'd ever worked.

I rang the technological and logistics expert as well as the chief information officer on our team, Decker Ashford, to inform him of the mission I was about to undertake.

"Grinder is in London now," he reported.

Of that, I was aware. He gave me the name of the same hotel where the man and I had met for a drink earlier that same day. I hated to interrupt what I knew was an inopportune time, but the third member of our team was currently in hospital, recovering from surgery.

I gave Ashford as much background as I had regarding the situation, asked him to determine the truest nature he could of the threat, and told him I'd check back once I made contact with Grinder.

Again, if it were anyone but the Queen herself asking me to do this, I would not make use of the SOS we used only for true emergencies, but I had no choice.

I made another call while I waited in the lobby for Grinder to join me, this time to Kensington's mother.

As expected, it went directly to voicemail, reinforcing my doubt that her daughter had actually been abducted.

"What is it?" Grinder asked when he exited the lift.

"A possible kidnapping."

He scrubbed his face with his hand. "Who?"

"Someone with close ties to the monarchy."

"We're going deep on this one, aren't we?"

"We are."

He looked over his shoulder at the lift and then back at me. "Let's go."

"Is there something you need to take care of first?"

When he shook his head, I wanted to suggest that he go up to the room and, at a minimum, tell the woman whose bed he'd just left that he was leaving London. However, that would require I explain how I knew he'd been in said bed.

"There's been a sighting in Budapest," Decker reported a few minutes later. "I'm tracking credit cards and facial recognition."

"Did she appear to be in distress?" I asked, not surprised in the least by her whereabouts.

"The information didn't indicate either way, but I'll keep you informed of anything else I learn."

"Budapest?" Grinder asked.

"The plane is at Gatwick."

"Why Budapest?"

I told him what I'd heard about Kensington's involvement with the heir to the former Austro-Hungarian throne.

"Otto or Konstantine?"

"Konstantine," I responded, surprised Grinder knew anything of the historic empire.

"He's an asshole."

When we landed at the airport in Budapest at three in the morning and deplaned, a car was waiting on the tarmac.

"Who *are* you?" Grinder asked facetiously. "And more importantly, can you arrange for a cup of tea and something to eat?"

I was the nephew of a reigning monarch, a king, and I could arrange for anything Grinder or I wanted, any time, day or night. Did I take advantage of my position? As little as possible with the exception of keeping the Bombardier at my disposal.

A driver delivered us to the Four Seasons Hotel where he'd already checked in on our behalf, under assumed names, and in the penthouse suite. With three bedrooms and a private lift, it would give us a place to set up a makeshift command center while affording us ultimate privacy.

"How much money do the Invincibles have?" asked Grinder, looking at the view from the suite's window.

"You receive monthly reports."

He raised a brow.

"Upwards of forty million pounds sterling. Do you require an exact number?" He certainly shouldn't. Grinder was wealthy without his stake in the Invincibles.

"Wow," he said, looking at the screen of his mobile. I opened mine as well and perused the same photos of Kensington that I assumed he was. "She's gorgeous."

Breathtakingly so. Despite the fact that Miss Whitby was far too young for me, I felt a stirring. Two, in fact. The first was one of intense attraction; the second, the same level of inappropriate possessiveness. Both were equally ridiculous. However, the longer Grinder studied the images on his mobile, the more I found myself wanting to rip it from his hand.

She looked like the supermodel her familial connections would never allow her to be. She was tall, perhaps close to six feet. She was reed-thin but with ample breasts, evident in the photo of her in a hot-pink bikini. Her honey-blonde hair was waist-length, and her amber-colored eyes were beguiling.

I'd seen her only once before, when she was a child. She was no longer anything of the sort.

"No wonder Konstantine was intrigued."

"Given he no longer has royal connections and Kensington very much does, he's in over his head. Not to mention, with the death of her grandmother, she inherited a significant amount of money."

"Do you think he kidnapped her?"

"What I think is irrelevant. Her Majesty the Queen, whom we both serve, believes it to be true; therefore, we will act accordingly."

"What if we locate her and she's unwilling to come with us?"

"I sincerely hope it doesn't come to that."

We slept for a few hours while we waited for further word on whether Kensington or Konstantine had been spotted again. It was late in the evening by the time we did.

"Decker said she was seen by the same person who spotted her previously," said Grinder, reading something on his mobile. "She's in the seventh district."

I groaned inwardly, familiar with the area known for a perpetual party atmosphere. I rubbed my chest against the feeling that overcame me—Kensington was not there of her own free will. "Let's go."

2

Kensington
Budapest

I would've left hours ago if two things hadn't happened. First, Konstantine was drunk. While I normally wouldn't care, I'd recently witnessed him become unreasonably angry when inebriated. Rather than risk his ire, it was easier for me to stick around and remain bored out of my wits.

Second, I'd noticed a hulking figure hovering at random times tonight. We'd been to three different clubs, and I saw him at each. At first, I thought perhaps he was a bodyguard I hadn't yet met. That still may be the case, but I wasn't about to go off on my own and be wrong.

I rested my elbow on the table and propped my head on my hand. Konstantine looked over his shoulder at me. When his eyes scrunched, I did my best to perk up.

The only reason I'd agreed to accompany him to Budapest in the first place, was because I was bored. Ironic that now I was more so.

I wanted to roll my eyes when he approached and sat beside me.

"You do not like my friends, Kenzie?"

I gave him my best fake smile. "Of course I do. I'm a bit tired is all." We had been drinking for several hours; not something I made a habit of.

"Perhaps you think you are better than we are?"

Oh no. I'd been witness to the ugliness that started with statements just like that. Unfortunately, I had no idea how to deflect his anger.

"I was hoping we could spend some time on our own, Konstantine."

As I'd hoped, his eyes pricked up. "Yeah?"

I nodded. To this point, I'd avoided having sex with him. I hope he bought my sudden change of heart.

"Let's go," he said, grabbing my hand and swaying as much as he slurred his words. He led me to the waiting car, stumbled as we got in, and fell on top of me. The smell of alcohol on his breath coupled with his behavior made me want to wretch.

I let him kiss me, but pulled away and motioned to the car's driver.

"He doesn't care. Do you, Boris?"

The man shook his head. "I do not, but the lady might."

When Konstantine surprised me and backed off, I wanted to climb into the front seat and kiss the driver.

Once back at the hotel, I helped Konstantine to the lift and then down the hallway to our room where I poured him another drink.

Rather than take it, he pushed me up against the wall, sending the glass of liquor flying across the room. Using both hands, he ripped the bodice of my dress.

"Konstantine! What in the bloody hell?" I shouted, trying to get away from where he had me pinned.

"You're a fucking tease, Kenzie, and I'm sick of it. Enough games. By tomorrow evening, you'll be my wife and mine to do with as I please."

His wife? Was he as mad as he was drunk? I pushed him with all my might, and he stumbled into the sofa. I tried to get to the door, but he grabbed my arm and dug his fingers into my flesh. When I screamed for help, he spun me around with one arm and backhanded me with the other.

"You goddamn bitch," he seethed. "Shut your fucking mouth." He tried to kiss me again, and I bit his lip as hard as I could, tasting the metallic tang of blood. "You like it rough, princess? No problem."

He grabbed my throat and squeezed. I fought for air, knowing that, within seconds, I would lose consciousness and he'd either continue strangling me until I was dead, or he'd rape me.

I closed my eyes when dizziness overcame me, and felt my body giving way. "Gran Bea, help me," I muttered with what little voice I had left.

The door burst open, and two men rushed in. *"Let her go!"* one yelled. I slid down the wall, gasping for air as the other man tackled and restrained Konstantine.

The man who'd yelled, picked me up and rushed out of the room with me in his arms.

"He…he tried to rape me," I stuttered.

"Shh," he murmured, racing down the hallway with me still in his arms. "I've got you. You're safe."

By the time the door to the lift opened, the other man had joined us. "Here," he said, covering me with a blanket. "How is she?" he asked.

The man holding me didn't respond.

We took the lift, and when the doors opened, he went in the opposite direction of the lobby, to a back exit where I saw an SUV just outside. Someone opened the passenger door, and the man holding me set me on the seat, made sure the blanket covered me, and then climbed in. He put his arm around my shoulders and held me close when I started to cry. "You're safe now."

The vehicle sped off and then slowed a few minutes later when we pulled into the driveway of another hotel.

"Come," the man said once it stopped by the entrance. He lifted me from the seat and into his arms. There was something about him so familiar, but given my mental state, I may not have recognized my own mother.

"Who are you?" I whispered as we waited for the lift.

He looked over at a couple waiting. "I'll explain everything once we're upstairs."

I squirmed out of his arms, and he set me on my feet. There was no way I was going up to a hotel room with a man I didn't know. It was bad enough I'd gotten into a car with him. Where was my head? Konstantine had just tried to rape me, and here I was, allowing a man to just carry me about without me giving another thought for my own safety—it didn't matter that he was charming, handsome, or that he smelled bloody fantastic. Lots of criminals did.

I turned my back and wrapped the blanket around me so I could hold it closed.

He didn't say anything until the couple got on the lift and the door closed behind them. "My name is Cortez DeLéon. Someone who knew your grandmother, was concerned for your safety and asked me to find you."

The name sounded familiar, but I couldn't place it. "Who are you?" I repeated.

"I have experience with locating missing persons."

I liked that he didn't repeat his name, but instead, understood I'd meant something different. "Was it the Queen?"

He didn't answer, but I knew it was. Who else could snap their fingers and have someone look for me? Not that I'd been lost.

"How did you know…" My voice trailed off when the other man joined us.

"Hi," he said, holding out his hand. "No time to introduce myself earlier." He smiled. "I'm Grinder."

"Kensington." I shook his hand.

The lift chimed, the doors opened, and a group of people got out before we got in. The man who'd introduced himself as Cortez hit the button to close the door before anyone else could get on.

The name sounded as familiar as he seemed, but I couldn't place it.

When he put a card in the slot and pressed the button marked "PH," the lift began its ascent. The doors reopened, and we stepped off directly into the suite.

"Grinder will order food. After you eat, you may rest."

"Um…I'm sorry I don't know what to call you."

"Call him Rile."

"Cortez is fine." He put his hand on the small of my back and ushered me over to a sitting area. "What would you like to eat?"

"I'm not hungry."

"You will feel better if you have food in your stomach." He smiled at me in a way a father might at his daughter, but the feeling that came over me was nothing like a child would feel for a parent. While the other man was probably closer to my age, it was Cortez who'd claimed my interest.

There was no hair on his head, but the stubble on his chin was gray, and he had the bluest eyes. Something about his powerful hands as he held me earlier and guided me now, his broad shoulders and strong arms, made me feel safe, even though both men had an intimidating aura about them.

There was something I'd wanted to ask him, but having him this close made me a little dizzy. He smelled so good. There was something familiar about his scent. What was it?

"How do you know the Queen?" I asked instead when I couldn't remember my original question.

"I am a relative."

"I…um…don't have my clothes."

Cortez closed and opened his bright blue eyes slowly. "I'll have it taken care of. There is a robe in the closet you may wear for now." He pointed toward a doorway.

"Are you going back to the other hotel?"

He studied me for a moment and then shook his head. "No."

"How, then, will you get my clothes?"

Again, he studied me. "Trust me."

I'd never felt more terrified in my life than when Konstantine was attacking me, but there was something about this man that made me smile. It also sent tingles down my spine.

"I'd like to bathe." I wanted to scrub everywhere Konstantine had touched me.

Cortez nodded and closed the door when I stepped into the room.

I sunk down in the warm water of the tub. I was so strung out that I thought I might fall to sleep straight away if I wasn't careful.

I washed my hair, scrubbed my body, drained the tub, and filled it a second time. I rested my back against the cool porcelain and closed my eyes. With the tub's depth, the water came close to my neck, and it felt bloody wonderful.

Despite my resolve not to, I must've drifted off, but woke when I heard a knock on the door.

"Dinner has arrived," Cortez said in a loud voice.

"I'll be right there," I hollered back.

I hadn't felt hungry earlier, but once the scents of goulash and *stropachka* wafted into the room, I hurriedly grabbed the robe from the closet.

"It smells fantastic," I said, taking a seat in the chair Cortez held for me. Before sitting back down, he set a dish in front of me.

"There is more, and we can always order something else if this doesn't suit."

I couldn't help but notice the look on Grinder's face, although I couldn't read it. Amusement perhaps?

Cortez sat beside me. "Would you like a glass of wine?"

"Please." I took two heaping bites of the goulash and the noodles that reminded me of German spaetzle.

"I have received a request that we accompany you to your mother's house," Cortez said a few minutes later.

My eyes remained focused on my food. "That won't be necessary."

"That we accompany you?" Grinder asked.

"No. She'd rather not go to her mother's," Cortez said before I had a chance to respond. It suddenly dawned on me who he was, although it didn't explain why the Queen had asked him to come looking for me.

"You're King Ferdinand's nephew."

Cortez nodded.

"Then, you should be aware I'll be fine once we've returned to England. The monarchy provides security." A look passed between the two men. "What?"

"There may be some retaliation," Grinder answered; Cortez glared at him. "What?" he asked like I had.

"Her Majesty has made the suggestion."

He emphasized the word in such a way that I knew it was nothing of the kind. The Queen was demanding I go to America—to my mother's house.

"What about my father?" I'd much prefer staying with him until my great-aunt deemed it safe for me to return home.

Cortez reached out and covered my hand with his. "I regret what you've just gone through. I will do my best to make the arrangements you'd prefer."

Again, I couldn't help but notice Grinder's reaction. This time, he appeared incredulous.

It was my own reaction that bothered me more. I found myself wanting to crawl into Cortez's lap and have him kiss me.

"Excuse me." Before I could push my chair back, Cortez stood to pull it out for me, looking at me questioningly.

"I'm very tired. I'd like to rest now if that would be okay."

"Of course. Do you need anything else before you retire?"

"I don't think so." Clothes, but he'd said he'd take care of that.

"Rile." Grinder pointed toward another door.

"Right." He rushed over to a closet and removed several hanging items, all covered in garment sleeves. With his other hand, he picked up two bags. "If you'll give me a moment, I'll bring the rest."

"What is all this?" I asked when he returned with more.

"Clothes. And shoes, of course."

"I may need a few more things."

He looked at me with wide eyes. "Like?"

"I'm joking." Even I was surprised at my ability to do so, given what I'd been through with that bastard Konstantine. "Thank you, Cortez. I appreciate this gesture very much."

"You'll find something to sleep in." He motioned with his arm in the direction of the bags he'd set around the room.

"I'm sure I'll find something for every conceivable occasion."

"Rest well," he said after studying me for long enough that it made me want to ask him to stay. He walked out and closed the door behind him, leaving me wishing I'd been brave enough to ask him not to go.

3

Rile

"Do you want to explain?"

I'd anticipated this. "Kensington has been through a tremendous ordeal. There's nothing more to be done tonight."

"Nothing more to be done? What about Konstantine?"

"Why would you assume that isn't already being taken care of?" Not in the way I would've preferred. However, I did not intend to share the specifics with Grinder. He would be as displeased as I, but far more likely to act on it. Doing so would not help matters. It was up to Konstantine's father to see to it his son was properly dealt with.

He walked over to the bar area. "Brandy?"

"Please."

"Who is she to you?"

"What do you mean?"

"I've never seen you act this way around anyone." Grinder handed me the glass. "She makes you nervous."

"That's absurd."

"Not in the least. You are typically the quintessential gentleman. You charm women in a way I may have once envied, but with her, you're tongue-tied."

"I'm nothing of the sort." I would admit, only to myself, that there was something about Kensington that rankled. It was almost as though she could read me in a way few could. No one, really. There had been someone capable once, but she was gone, never to be replaced.

I drained the brandy in the glass and set it on the bar. "I believe I'll retire as well." I went into the room next to the one where Kensington slept, and closed the door. I pulled a book from my bag and settled on the bed without removing my clothes. If the woman on the other side of the wall needed something in the night, I wouldn't want her to be made uncomfortable, given I typically slept in the nude.

I'd drifted to sleep with the light on when I woke to whimpering sounds. I raced into the next room; Kensington was in the midst of a nightmare. I sat on the edge of the bed and stroked her hair until she came awake.

"You had a bad dream," I explained when she opened her eyes and looked into mine. She scooted over, not seemingly to get away from me, though. "Would you like me to stay until you are able to fall back asleep?"

"Would you mind terribly?"

"Not at all." I rested my back against the headboard, stunned when Kensington burrowed under my arm and rested her head on my chest.

"You seem so familiar," she murmured, half asleep.

"We met once. It's been years now. Perhaps that's what you're remembering."

"No. That isn't it."

It seemed only a matter of minutes before her breathing evened out, and I knew she was asleep. Rather than easing out from under her, I closed my eyes.

When I woke and checked the time, it was close to eight in the morning. In her sleep, Kensington had rolled away from me, so I gently rose from the bed and quietly opened and closed the door behind me. I looked up and saw Grinder seated at the same table where we'd had a late dinner the night before.

"Tea?" he asked with a smirk.

"In a moment." I went into the bedroom and to the lavatory. I needed a shower and a shave but would see to it once I'd had my morning tea.

"She had a bad dream," I explained when I came back out to join him.

"You owe me no explanation."

"I feel as though I do. Your judgment is stifling."

He laughed. "She mentioned preferring to stay with her father."

"Yes," I muttered, not looking forward to telling her that staying with him would not be an option, given I'd not heard back from him, even after leaving an urgent message.

"What's the story there?"

"Her father is Michael Alexander Whitby."

"Whit?"

I nodded. "You know him."

"Of him, and that makes sense. I hadn't put it together. Isn't he a famous wildlife photographer?"

"I believe so."

"And her mum?"

"Kiki Buckley." Kendra Astor Whitby Buckley, more accurately. Former débutante of the year, present socialite of equal merit, alcoholic, adulteress, and a ghastly parent. I couldn't fault Kensington for not wanting to stay with her. "Kensington's grandparents raised her in England."

I didn't know either well, but everything I'd heard indicated that William "Huck" Huxly Whitby and his wife, Beatrice, the sister of the Queen's consort, were very good to their granddaughter.

"Are there no other options?"

I shook my head. Both Whit and Kiki were only children, so there were no aunts or uncles with whom Kensington could reside—other than the Queen, her great-aunt, and staying with her was not an option.

Not to mention, she was a grown woman, an adult who had lived on her own since her grandmother's death several months ago.

"She's twenty-six?" Grinder asked, looking at something on his laptop.

"That's right."

"Seems younger."

I brushed my lower lip with my finger. "As I said earlier, your judgment is stifling."

"Whenever you do that thing with your lip, it's like you're either reading someone's mind or you're getting a message from the '*great beyond.*'"

He had no idea the accuracy of his words, not that I would ever admit it to him or anyone else.

When the bedroom door opened, Grinder and I both stood.

"Good morning, Kensington."

She padded over when I pulled the chair out for her. "Tea?"

"Yes, please. When did you leave?" she asked when Grinder excused himself.

"Not more than an hour ago." I looked into her amber-colored eyes, studied the perfect features of her face. She looked so young without makeup.

"Thank you for staying with me."

I almost slipped and said it was my pleasure, which it was, but it would be a completely inappropriate thing for me to say.

Grinder walked over to the lift when it chimed and ushered a gentleman in who was wheeling what I assumed was breakfast. He removed the plate covers, revealing pastries, strudel, muesli, and fruit.

"Go ahead," I said when Kensington eyed the strudel. She plucked it from the plate with a childlike smile. I leaned closer. "Feeling better this morning?"

"Since having gone to hell and back, you mean?"

From behind her, Grinder pointed at himself and then at the bedroom. I motioned with my head for him to join us.

"Mind a little sunshine?" he asked, walking over to the draperies.

Once opened, the light provided me a better look at the side of Kensington's face. It was all I could do not to reach over and stroke her cheek with my fingertip.

"Bloody wanker backhanded me," she mumbled, noticing my gaze.

I felt a rage building inside of me; I stood and excused myself into the bedroom. I closed the door, walked into the en suite, and threw water on my face like I had earlier. I sat on the edge of the bed and took several deep breaths. When I closed my eyes, I could see Konstantine attacking her. A roar of anger burned in my chest that I pushed back down. I heard a light tap at the door.

"Come in."

Kensington eased the door open, but stood on the threshold. "I'm sorry."

"You've nothing to be sorry for."

"You're angry."

I turned my back, but I could still see her face in the mirror. In this light, the bruises were even more pronounced.

"He was very drunk."

I nodded, wishing she didn't feel as though she had to make excuses for the man who'd attacked her.

She looked as if she was struggling with what to say next. "Um, I don't have my mobile."

"I'll take care of it."

"Cortez?"

I turned around and studied her.

"I'd rather not go to Kiki's."

I understood, I just didn't have an alternative. And I had no choice but to abide by the Queen's request that she go to America for the time being.

When she left and closed the door behind her, I made arrangements for us to travel to London and then on to the States.

From the moment we left the hotel, Kensington's demeanor changed from timid to agitated. When we boarded the plane and I asked her to take a seat, she did so with folded arms and a scowl on her face. I sat in the spot closest to her.

I was about to threaten her with taking her over my knee and spanking her like I would a child with similar behavior, but I took several deep breaths instead when it resulted in my body's highly inappropriate reaction.

I closed my eyes and imagined Kensington on her knees, hands on my thighs, eyes imploring as she begged me to forgive her. It took my breath away. In my vision, her hands moved from where they rested on my trousers to my belt. Instead of allowing her to continue, I pulled her to her feet, cupped her luscious bottom with both my hands, and punished her with my kiss.

The hitch of her breath jarred me out of my fantasy, and I opened my eyes.

Her eyes looked from mine to my lips. Her breathing was labored, and her cheeks were flushed in a way they might be if she could read my thoughts.

"How old are you, Cortez?"

"I will be thirty-seven next month."

She turned her head and looked out the window. "You seem older."

4

Kensington

I inwardly laughed at how my best friend, Teagon, had once taken the piss out of me when I told her I fancied a man we'd seen at the pub—who upon closer inspection appeared older than my father.

"Ew," she'd said. "What's with you and the daddy complex?"

"He's handsome and…distinguished-looking."

She'd taken another look. "God, Kenzie, he's my boss' boss."

I wondered what Teagon would think of Cortez. He was only ten years older than me. Plus a couple of months. Maybe I did have a daddy complex, given how much I wished he'd kiss me right now. He was thinking about it too, I could tell by the look on his face. I didn't let my eyes wander *south* to find out what else he might be thinking about.

What was wrong with me? I'd nearly been raped, and yet I was fantasizing about sex with Cortez.

He rested his arm near me, and I could see a tattoo sleeve peeking out from the cuff of his button-down shirt. There was something so sexy about a man like him having a sleeve. He seemed so formal, so proper, but obviously, he had an adventurous side.

He leaned closer. He smelled so bloody good, I couldn't help but take a deep breath.

"We'll fly to London. From there, we'll take another plane to America," he told me.

"Will you be traveling with me?"

"Yes, as will Grinder."

"Is that really his name?"

Cortez smiled. "His name is Miles Stone."

I understood what relation the name had with his, but not why it was necessary to call him something other than Miles.

"They call you Rile?"

"Yes."

I smiled when he didn't offer any explanation.

"Do you work for the Queen?"

"I do not."

"SIS?"

"At one time, yes."

"But not any longer?"

He shook his head.

"I meant to thank you for my clothes. I'll see to it you're reimbursed once we arrive in London."

"That won't be necessary."

"I insist," I pressed.

"And I insist you not." I was drawn to his lips when he smiled. I wished he'd kiss me, but I knew he wouldn't. He probably saw me as a nuisance—like a younger sister. I sighed and looked away in embarrassment.

He put his finger on my chin and turned my head so I faced him. His eyes studied mine, and for a moment, I was certain he could read my thoughts. He ran his fingertip over my cheek where Konstantine had hit me.

"Does it hurt?" he asked.

"No," I answered, hoping he wouldn't stop.

"I hate that he did this to you," he murmured.

When I leaned forward, my mouth close to his, he dropped his hand and leaned back.

"Excuse me." He stood and walked toward the back of the plane, leaving me feeling bereft and mortified.

I put my head in my hands and turned my body so I was facing the plane's window.

When the aircraft landed, I stood as soon as it came to a stop on the tarmac. I knew the Queen wanted me to go to America, but I simply couldn't allow Cortez to accompany me. I'd call her and beg her to let me either stay in England or to travel to my mother's on my own.

"Kensington, wait." Cortez stepped in front of me and barred my exit.

"Please," I implored. "Let me pass."

He gently took my arm and moved me out of the way so Grinder could depart the plane. We waited there until the crew left as well.

"Kensington...I find myself...perhaps I've given you the wrong impression."

My cheeks flamed. This was precisely the thing I wanted to avoid. "No. You did nothing of the sort. Please, may I get off the plane now?"

He didn't budge. Instead, he cupped my cheek with his palm. "I find myself..." he repeated. "Unable to resist." He brought his lips to mine and kissed me. It was softer, gentler, and far sexier than any other kiss I'd ever experienced. His tongue caressed my bottom lip, and I opened my mouth to him.

Oh, but this man could kiss. He angled his head, his tongue stroking mine, and my knees weakened. I never wanted him to stop, but he did.

"I'm—"

I put my fingers on his lips, knowing he was about to apologize, and I couldn't bear it. I skirted around him and rushed down the steps, across the tarmac, and into the private terminal, hoping to be able to get to a phone to call my great-aunt. As I went through the second set of double doors, I immediately recognized several of the security agents who stood between me and the hallway leading to the public terminals.

"The other plane is right this way," said Grinder, motioning for me to go ahead.

"I'll just stop in the ladies' first."

"You may make use of the one on the plane."

"Very well," I muttered. "But I must hurry."

He escorted me onto the plane and motioned toward the forward loo.

"I'm sorry, is there a stateroom?" This wasn't my first ride on a private plane, let alone one like this. I recognized straight away how best to avoid further embarrassment by having to face Cortez.

"There is."

I looked to my right and saw the man himself walking across the tarmac. "May I?"

"Of course."

I shut the door behind me and locked it before going in to use the loo. It dawned on me then that Cortez had said he'd take care of getting my mobile. Or did he mean "a mobile."

My handbag was also back in Konstantine's hotel room along with my passport and credit cards. *Dammit.* What a headache it would be to replace all that, particularly from America. I flopped on the bed and rolled over, burying my face in the pillow. What a bloody mess my life was, all because I'd gone off with Konstantine von Habsburg on a stupid whim.

There was a rap at the door, but I didn't answer until I heard Grinder's voice. I opened it a crack. "Yes?"

"Here you are." He handed me my bag.

"How did you…never mind."

"Your clothes, the ones you brought to Budapest, are in the hold with your other luggage."

"Thank you."

He looked as though he had something else to say, so I waited. "He won't bite, you know."

"I've no clue what you mean."

He smiled. "Sure, you don't. Buckle up for takeoff."

The first person I called when my mobile powered up was my father.

"Hey, baby girl. How are you?"

"I'm on my way to stay with Kiki."

He laughed. "That says it all, doesn't it?"

"I'd rather come stay with you, Daddy."

"I've heard through the 'chain of command' that my aunt has requested you go to America, darling."

"Where are you now?"

"The Atacama Desert in Chile."

"That's South America. Wouldn't it count?"

My father laughed again. "I'm certain it would not. To be honest, it's almost a miracle you were able to reach me. There's literally no mobile service where I am."

"Must be a sign that I was meant to speak with you."

"Anyway, stay well, darling. You are well-versed in avoiding your mother. I have faith you will see as little of her on this visit as you would've any other time of your life."

The same could be said of him, but confronting him now would not accomplish anything. I'd been lucky that I was able to live with my grandparents throughout my childhood.

I'd hidden myself away in the stateroom, locked the door, and yet I was still disappointed that an hour passed and Cortez hadn't knocked on the door.

I stretched out and hoped to sleep, but tossed and turned instead. It occurred to me how selfish I'd been to take the stateroom without asking if either Cortez or Grinder would like to make use of it.

I stood, straightened my clothes, grabbed my bag, and opened the door. Cortez was seated just outside and bolted upright.

"Is anything wrong?"

He startled me, and I put my hand on my heart. "No. I just thought someone else might want to rest."

He scrubbed his face with his hand. "You're avoiding me."

I saw that Grinder was obviously asleep, based on the way his mouth hung open, so I sat down beside Cortez. "I'm embarrassed. That's all."

"Because I kissed you?"

"Because you wish you hadn't."

"It's not—"

I put my fingertips on his lips. "Please do not tell me that it's you, not me, or anything equally trite. I wanted you to kiss me, and you did. So, thank you."

He moved my fingers away from his lips but held onto my hand and smiled. "I can assure you, the pleasure was all mine." He sighed. "Kensington."

"Yes?"

"It's a beautiful name."

Mixed signals much?

He dropped my hand. "I'm confusing you. It's unfair." He motioned to the stateroom. "Rest. It's a long flight."

"I doubt I'll sleep anyway. You go ahead."

"What if I sit with you until you're able to sleep?"

"I do remember you."

He raised an eyebrow.

"I remember the way you smelled."

We both laughed. When Cortez stood and held out his hand, I rested mine in it. We went into the room, and he pulled out the bunk. It was much bigger than I thought, more like a king-size bed than the full I'd expected.

"My father's plane has a much nicer stateroom," he murmured, perhaps by way of an apology.

"Whose plane is this?"

"It is also part of the DeLéon fleet."

Something told me this wasn't information he shared with just anyone, or easily.

Cortez put his strong arm around me, and I nestled into him, just like I had last night in the hotel room. Within minutes, I felt myself drifting to sleep.

5

Rile

It seemed my body was ignoring every message my brain was sending it as though the connection was lost. My only saving grace was that, within hours, we would arrive in America and Kensington would be safely ensconced with her mother.

I knew I shouldn't kiss her, yet I did. I knew I shouldn't tease her, yet I did. I knew I shouldn't be lying on this bed with her in my arms, yet I was.

A warm feeling settled over me as I rested my head against hers, smiling that she recalled the way I smelled.

"She's good for you," came the voice.

I shook my head. *She's too young for me. I represent someone who protected her, saved her. There's nothing more to it.*

"Open your heart, Cort. It's time."

It wasn't time. It would never be time. Regardless of how much the voice in my head pushed me, reopening my heart would never happen. *Your death destroyed me, Celestina. It broke my heart, and there is no way to repair it.*

"This one will repair it, Cort. Trust me."

I eased from under Kensington's sleeping form and quietly left the stateroom. Twenty-four hours from now, Kensington would be someone I rescued, like I had so many others. She wouldn't be part of my life any more than they were.

"Are you going to be like this for the rest of the flight?" Grinder asked.

"Like what?"

"Sullen. Argumentative. A pain in the arse."

"I am none of those things." Especially the first.

He grunted and moved to a seat near the front of the aircraft. I stayed in the middle, and Kensington was fast asleep in the aft. Social-distancing at its finest, I thought with a smile. Keeping people at arm's length was a specialty of mine. Any closer, and losing them would hurt more than I could bear. One loss alone had nearly destroyed me. More, I'd never live through.

When the pilot announced our initial descent into White Plains Airport, I returned to the stateroom to find Kensington awake and sitting in one of the chairs.

"I was just about to come out," she said, putting something I couldn't see in her bag.

"Very well," I said, turning to leave.

"Cortez?"

"Yes?"

"Have you spoken with Kiki?"

"I have not."

She looked away, toward the window. "She may not appreciate my showing up."

"She was the one who alerted the Queen, Kensington. I'm sure it was out of concern for the daughter she would like very much to protect from harm." As I recalled, though, the Queen had said she believed the news came by way of Kensington's mother. It now occurred to me that it hadn't been from her mother at all, it had been from mine.

Kensington laughed and shook her head. "Concern and protect are two words that have never been in my mother's vocabulary."

I rested my hand on the jamb of the stateroom door when I felt the essence of a hand on my shoulder.

"She needs you," came the unwelcome voice I'd heard enough from earlier.

"We'll land shortly. Grinder and I will accompany you to your mother's residence." I abruptly turned and walked away, knowing by my glimpse of the look on her face that Kensington felt my harsh dismissal. Rather than try to make up for it, I returned to my seat.

Kensington was understandably subdued when we arrived at her mother's residence in Greenwich, Connecticut. The stately home was one of the few remaining Long Island Sound compounds, large enough both in square footage and acreage that Kensington and her mother could live on the estate and never see one another. It was in gate-guarded Indian Harbor and sat almost directly on an expansive shoreline, making it more secure than many of the area's other communities.

As we drove through the gates of the estate, we passed verdant landscaped grounds, a pool, tennis court, and putting green.

"You can pull in there," Kensington said, pointing to what looked to be a guest house.

"We'll stop at the main residence first," I said to the driver before he made the turn.

The front door was open, and we stepped inside, but Kiki was nowhere to be seen.

"I hate this place," Kensington muttered under her breath.

Even I had to admit its ostentatiousness was overwhelming. The entryway alone was ornate to the point of being gaudy. Buckingham Palace had nothing on this.

"There you are." A woman I wouldn't have recognized had we not been in her home, approached from the back of the house. "Hello, darling." She cheek-kissed Kensington, put both hands on her shoulders, and took a step back. "You look exhausted. I've warned you, the lifestyle you lead will catch up with you if you don't take care."

"Hi, Kiki."

In three sentences and one look about, I understood why Kensington didn't want to be here.

"Cortez! Goodness, I didn't see you there." My eyes met Kensington's as her mother walked toward me, and I winked.

"Hello, Kiki. May I introduce my associate Miles Stone?"

"Aren't you a handsome one?" she said to him, cheek-kissing him after me. "Kenzie, don't you think Mr. Stone is handsome?"

"How many times must I remind you, Mother? I am a lesbian."

"Oh, pish-posh with that. I know you say that simply to get me riled up."

Again, my eyes met Kensington's, and we both smiled.

"What about you, Cortez?" Kiki's voice changed from sing-songy to solemn. "I was so sorry to hear—"

"It's been years, Kiki. No need to offer condolences now."

"Has it been that long? Well, I certainly hope someone else has snapped you up. Connected to royalty via your father and your mother—goodness, but you're a catch. If I weren't already married…Too bad Kenzie is so young. What can I bring you? It's early for a martini, but you have been traveling so, *c'est la vie,* as they say."

I hadn't seen Kiki in years, but still, I should've remembered how she was. I couldn't regret bringing her daughter here more. Would that I could rewind time and keep her with me in England.

God! What was I thinking? Keep her in England with me? Had I forgotten my resolve to deliver her to her mother and then walk away?

"Thank you for the offer, Kiki, but we cannot stay."

"What? But you've just arrived."

"Kensington has just arrived. We were merely her escorts."

"I've a mind to figure out a way to force you to stay, but never mind. Go if you must. Kenzie, where are your things?"

"Still in the car, Kiki. I'll be staying in the guest house."

Her mother folded her arms. I was anxious to hear what she'd come up with in order to save face. I'm sure where Kensington stayed mattered little to her other than for appearances.

"Perhaps you'll be able to catch up on your sleep if you do, darling."

"Thanks, Mother," she said and turned to me. "If you wouldn't mind having your driver drop my bags. I'll walk from here."

"If you'll give me a moment to say goodbye to Kiki, I'll go with you."

"Not necessary, but thank you."

She walked out of the room, leaving me unable to follow without making a scene.

"What about your younger brother, Cortez? Wouldn't he suit Kenzie?"

"He's happily married, I'm afraid."

"Disappointing, that one." She motioned in the direction Kensington had left. "I thought Konstantine von Habsburg was a good match, but she obviously didn't make much of an impression on him."

"We really must be going," I heard Grinder say as I took ten deep breaths in an attempt to stop myself from strangling the woman standing in front of me.

Didn't make much of an impression? The wanker tried to rape her. Before I could stop myself, I heard the words coming out of my own mouth in a tone that could only be construed as angry. "Did you or did you not contact the Queen and tell her your daughter had been kidnapped?"

Kiki's eyes opened wide. "I did nothing of the sort! As if I'd have access to the Queen. How absurd. Until I received your message saying you were on your way here with her, I assumed she was off gallivanting the way she always does. What happened with von

Habsburg, anyway? Is there any hope things might work out between him and Kenzie?"

"Had we not arrived when we did, your daughter would've been brutally raped, or worse."

"Surely, she exaggerates." Kiki took a step back, and I took a step forward.

"Time for us to go," reminded Grinder. "We have a flight to catch."

There was no flight, but he was right to urge me to leave. Nothing good could come of a confrontation between Kensington's mother and me.

I turned and walked out without the civility of a goodbye, too angry to do anything but. I waited in the car while Grinder, I hoped, gave his regrets and smoothed things over.

"We have to get her away from here," I said when Grinder got in the car.

"You were the one insisting she come."

I glared at him. Recriminations were unwelcome, given I had no idea what fresh hell we were delivering Kensington to.

As we drove to the guest house, I looked for Kensington. While the driver unloaded her bags, I went to the front door and knocked. Hearing nothing, I tried the handle and found it open like that of the main house. "Kensington?" I called out.

"There she is," said Grinder, coming in behind me and pointing toward the water.

I knew from the long hair blowing in the wind that the woman speeding away from the estate, alone in a motorboat, was her.

"Let's go," I snapped.

"Edge has been released and is on his way to Texas," Grinder said, looking at his phone on the drive back to the airfield. "Lynx is with him."

"We'll meet them there."

We'd been on a mission in China three months ago with Lynx, Edge's older brother, during which the younger Edgemon was shot.

In the midst of what seemed an easy in-and-out op, we were met by a hail of bullets moments before we left the building with the agents we'd been hired to extract. Edge was the only one of us hit. A bullet had penetrated his right arm, requiring three surgeries in order for him to regain full use of it.

It was Lynx I was most anxious to talk to. I'd made him an offer to join our firm, knowing perhaps better than he did himself, that he would soon make his permanent home in America. Currently a high-ranking MI6 officer, he was the perfect candidate to be the Invincible's managing partner for US operations.

Presently, we were comprised of four founding partners—myself, Grinder, Edge, and Decker. I had not intended to add a fifth partner until I intuited that Lynx might be available. Before making him the offer, though, I'd called a partners' meeting; the decision to proceed had been unanimous.

While I could've remained with MI6 until the end of my career, I had no desire to go further up the ranks. I much preferred the idea of working with independent agents, picking and choosing the missions we agreed to accept. It was with that idea I approached Decker Ashford first and then Grinder and Edge.

I named the firm the Invincible Intelligence and Security Group. My partners weren't enamored with it, but I was. There were few other instances I exercised power or authority as the founder of the firm. I suppose that's why they agreed to live with the name.

Decker's wife was the first to call us the Invincibles, back when our inaugural mission was to find her sister's killer. I doubted any of them would admit liking the moniker, but I sensed they did.

I was anxious to grow the firm and had several agents, officers, and independent operatives in mind to join us. Given several of those individuals were based in the States, I could use the time in Texas to set up meetings.

"You're deep in thought," said Grinder when we arrived at the airfield.

"Business."

"I thought you were going to get into it with Kiki."

"Yes," I murmured. "Thank you for preventing me from doing so."

"I wish there'd been an alternative."

As did I.

6

Rile

Grinder and I arrived at King-Alexander Ranch a few hours after leaving Kiki's, and were seated at the dining room table in the ranch's main residence. We were chatting with the ranch's owner, Quint Alexander, his wife, Darrow, and Decker Ashford, when Edge walked in with Lynx. I sensed something was wrong, but it wasn't with Edge himself, or Lynx.

I watched as Darrow, an MI6 agent in her own right, code name Shadow, greeted the two men.

When Edge turned to me, I stood and embraced him. I took a step back, held out my hand, and he shook it. "Good," I murmured. His grip was strong. "Back to normal?"

He nodded. "Mostly."

"You all right?" I heard Grinder ask him when they too embraced.

When Edge shook his head, I studied him, but still couldn't get a read on what was troubling him.

"Can I get you both a drink?" Quint asked.

"Please. If it's not an intrusion," Edge answered.

"Of course not."

The Invincibles team and I had spent many evenings on this ranch and at this table. Quint's father was Z Alexander, the current chief of MI6, and our former boss. While the ranch still belonged to Z, Quint had run it for years along with Decker Ashford, who Z had adopted out of foster care when he was a teenager.

"Lynx," I said, turning to him. "Do you have an answer for us?"

"Soon. I promise."

I watched as Edge leaned down and murmured something to Decker, who stood and followed him outside.

"What's going on?" Grinder asked Lynx.

"Something about the murder of a local man."

It wasn't long before Lynx left and Decker came back inside.

"There was a murder right before we left for the Chinese mission back in August. Edge believes he may have played a role in it."

"He didn't," I said.

Every head at the table turned to me. I couldn't explain why I was convinced he hadn't. As with so many things, it was a feeling.

"A woman was arrested and is currently in county lockup, awaiting trial. Edge says he knows she's innocent. I'll contact Mac at the sheriff's office in the morning and see what else I can find out. Edge plans to visit the jail tomorrow. He's contacting an attorney now to meet him there."

I was certain the woman who'd been arrested was innocent, like Edge believed, but this time, I'd keep my premonition to myself.

"The victim had ties to the Aryan Brotherhood of Texas," Decker reported the next morning. "Hammer was able to negotiate the release of the woman arrested for the murder, but there was a condition."

Sterling Anderson, aka Hammer, was an attorney with ties to the intelligence community, who just happened to live in this part of Texas.

"And that was?"

"She's being released into Edge's custody."

I closed my eyes and brushed my lower lip with my finger, processing the information I was foreseeing. The most logical assumption was that someone within the ABT or its parent organization, the Aryan Nation, had murdered the man. The other possibility was that a rival gang was responsible for his death. Either way, it would be difficult to prove who carried out the hit.

Hammer's best bet to get the woman exonerated was to find enough counter-evidence to prove her innocent, or at least to establish reasonable doubt.

In anticipation of Edge coming to me, asking for the Invincibles to take on this investigation, I made several calls.

The first was to a contact at the CIA, Sumner Copeland. Cope was a handler and would know if the agency had anyone inside either the Aryan Nation or the ABT. If not, we would need to get our own team in place as quickly as possible.

I took another look at the operatives I'd wanted to meet with while I was in the States. There was a good chance we'd need their help on this investigation. Later, I'd give Grinder a list and ask him to reach out to them.

"Smoke is inside the Aryan Nation," reported Cope when I asked if they had already anyone undercover. As far as operatives went, he was at the top of my list to recruit.

Broderick "Smoke" Torcher was a brilliant agent—a warrior, a renegade, and a bloody genius. There wasn't a single situation he couldn't step into and master. The man was older than me by a handful of years, making me believe he would be ready to retire from the agency, given the opportunity.

After my call with Cope ended, I compiled a list of names for Grinder. There were two women included, Calla "Casper" Rey and Siobhan "Siren" Gallagher. Casper was a former CIA agent who'd quit the company and gone independent when her husband, Beau Rey, was killed in what many believed had been friendly fire. However, the CIA wouldn't own it.

Siren was an active officer in Irish Military Intelligence. Recruiting her would be more difficult, but eventually, I would.

The first three men I added for Grinder to contact were Breckin "Ink" Ryan, Garrett "Rage" Williams, and Mick "Jagger" Reynolds. Ink would be ideal to infiltrate the ABT. Rage and Jagger would prove useful if we needed someone undercover in a rival gang.

If we were able to recruit any or all of this target group, the Invincibles would be capable of handling this investigation as well as take on any other mission presented to us—black ops or otherwise.

Given that no one on the list worked for MI6, I wouldn't piss off Z Alexander by luring away more of his best talent.

I'd once considered making Cope an offer, but his father was a high-profile US senator. Any job his son moved into would need to be equally high-profile. My prediction was that one day, he'd become the director of the intelligence bureau, perhaps even become a senator or presidential cabinet member. Regardless, it would be equally important to stay in Cope's good graces.

"Mornin', Rile," said Quint, walking into his kitchen.

"We are inconveniencing you."

Quint poured a cup of what looked like black sludge and joined me at the table. "I'd argue and tell you you weren't, but with you, I've come to realize you have a better idea of what I'm thinking before I do."

"His mum was the same way," said Darrow, joining us after pouring a cup of the same thing Quint had. "Don't turn your nose up until you've tasted it," she said, catching the look of disgust on my face.

"I have tasted it, and I'll stick with tea, thank you."

"What were you saying about Rile's mother?" Quint asked.

"Right. She's said to have a sixth sense." Darrow's eyes met mine as if to challenge me to deny the rumors. She smiled when I said nothing.

While not public knowledge, my mother, before marrying my father and becoming the Duchess of Soria, had been with SIS. She was credited with exposing the final two men in what came to be known as the Cambridge Five. Unlike the three others who had defected to the Soviet Union, Anthony "Johnson" Blunt and John "Liszt" Cairncross remained with SIS until a year after my mother joined MI6.

It was her "sixth sense," as Darrow called it, that put her onto Blunt and Cairncross, eventually leading them to confess to British Intelligence.

Right before my father proposed, the Queen had offered to make my mother a Dame of the Most Honorable Order of the Bath. However, given an impending marriage to the brother of the reigning Spanish monarch, my mother privately declined the honor. Had she accepted, she would've been made a dame before the age of twenty-five. That alone spoke to the significance of her contributions in the short time she was with SIS.

She quietly retired from duty and, eventually, gave birth to my younger brother and me. I would be lying if I said my mother hadn't pushed me into service.

My only regret in following in her footsteps was that joining SIS had led me to meet the one true love of my life only to lose her five years later. The pain of that loss was ever-present, deep in my soul. It hadn't diminished and never would.

Darrow reached over and covered my hand with hers. Perhaps she had her own sixth sense.

Unlike my mother, who'd married into the duchy, Darrow was born into it. Her oldest brother and good friend of mine had become Duke of Bedfordshire upon the death of their father. Thornton "Shiver" Whittaker had been an MI6 officer, slated to become chief. Instead, he and his wife, Orina, a former KGB assassin, had retired to Whittaker Abbey and were raising a family.

"I've gotta get back to work." Quint kissed Darrow's cheek and excused himself.

"How's your brother?"

"Which one—Shiver or Wilder?"

"Both, actually."

"Shiver's well. In fact, Orina is pregnant with their third child. And Wilder, as you know, married Quint's sister. They're all very happy back in Bedfordshire."

"Brilliant. Please give them my regards."

"Rile…I heard another rumor. This one was about you."

"You shouldn't believe everything you hear." In our world, that meant leave it alone.

"Very well," she said, standing, smiling, and kissing my cheek before leaving the same way her husband had.

***

It was mid-December by the time our team completed our investigation and exonerated the woman we all knew was the love of Edge's life.

We'd finally located the real killer after Edge and Casper had gone undercover into the Aryan Brotherhood of Texas. Unbeknown to us at the time, the FBI had also infiltrated the organization. I was livid upon finding out they were already inside, and didn't hesitate to let Cope know it.

"The right hand doesn't always inform the left of what it's doing," he told me.

"You're telling me you knew nothing about the bureau's involvement when your own man was inside the national organization?"

"Believe me, Rile, internal affairs is all over this."

The bureaucratic bullshit was a primary reason why I didn't miss my employment with SIS. It made me think of Smoke again, and wonder if he was as fed up as I was. Perhaps now would be a good time to contact him and ask him to work for the Invincibles.

We had one final meeting scheduled to hotwash the investigation. After that, I planned to return to Spain. Both Grinder and Edge were staying on in the States, so I would be traveling alone, and I welcomed it. I prized my solitude, and after a mission that had taken place over the course of two months—involving the entire team along with hired operatives—I was ready for some peace and quiet.

I'd just taken my bag to the car when my mobile rang with a call from Casper.

"Can I catch a ride to the airport with you? I just need to make a stop at the dining hall on our way out. If it isn't too much trouble."

Given I was headed to my home on the island of Mallorca where I planned to avoid all of humanity for at least a month, I was happy to oblige.

I was in the car, waiting for Casper, when my mobile rang with a call from my mother.

"Hello, Duchess."

"Cortez."

"Something's wrong."

"Yes, I fear it is. Where are you?"

"In America, headed home in two hours."

"Oh, good. I hoped I'd find you still in the States."

"Mother?"

"Yes, yes, I'm getting to it."

I closed my eyes and took a deep breath. "It's to do with Kensington, isn't it?"

"Yes, and I'm afraid it's terribly complicated."

7

Kensington

"Of course, Konstantine, you are more than welcome to spend the holiday here with us." My mother paused. "Oh, you're already here? That's brilliant. When shall we expect you?" She paused again. "Perfect. Just in time for afternoon cocktails."

I came around the corner when the call ended. "Have you lost your mind?"

My mother set her phone on the kitchen counter and folded her arms.

"Do you not understand he tried to rape me?"

"He tells a different story, Kenzie," she said, taking a sip of her martini and leveling a nasty gaze at me.

Of course she would take anyone's side over mine; it was the way it had always been with Kiki. I didn't have time to stop and wonder why, not now, with Konstantine on his way here.

"When is he arriving?"

"He's at the airport, waiting to clear customs. When he does arrive, I expect you to welcome him graciously, Kensington."

I wanted to scream at her, but I wanted to avoid Konstantine more. "I'll go freshen up."

She downed the remaining liquor in her glass. "I'm happy to hear you've had a change of heart."

"Which airport?"

"White Plains."

I rushed out of the main residence and ran toward the guest house. The man who'd attacked me was on his way here and would probably arrive within a half hour.

Not knowing what else to do, given the urgency of my situation, I called the number Cortez had programmed into my mobile, praying he'd answer.

"Kensington," he said before I heard it ring.

"I'm sorry to—"

"Stop. I've just received a report that Konstantine von Habsburg is in the States. He may very well be on his way to your mother's estate as we speak."

Had he not interrupted me, I would've told him that very thing. "The reason for my call."

"You are aware, then?"

"I am, and in fact, he'll be here as soon as he's able to clear customs."

"I'll ring you right back."

"Cortez?" *The bloody bastard ended the call!*

My mobile rang within minutes.

"I've bought us some time."

"What does that mean?"

"Von Habsburg will not be out of customs any time soon. Now, listen very carefully to what I want you to do. Do you have a vehicle at your disposal?"

"Yes."

"I want you to go directly to the Indian Harbor Heliport. Do you know it?"

"It's ten minutes away."

"Good. Perfect. Once you've arrived, ring me. I'm making arrangements now for someone to meet you there."

I changed my clothes, pulled my hair back, and threw as much of my stuff as I could into a bag. I looked into the lavatory mirror and took several deep breaths before doing one more check to be certain I had my mobile, wallet, and passport before rushing to the garage. Thankfully, I didn't have to pass the main house to get there.

"Hello, Miss Kensington," said Thomas, one of my mother's chauffeurs. "Can I give you a lift somewhere?"

"As a matter of fact…"

Not more than twenty minutes after my call with Cortez ended, the driver pulled up to the heliport.

"Thank you so much for getting me here so quickly, Thomas. I have one more favor to ask." I reached into my wallet. "I'd rather my mother not be made aware of my departure."

He held up his hand rather than out when I tried to hand him some money. "Say no more, Miss Kensington. I haven't seen or heard from you in several days."

"Please, Thomas, take this."

He shook his head. "Be on your way, Miss."

I leaned over the seat and kissed his cheek.

As Thomas carried my bag inside the small lobby despite my protests that I could handle it on my own, I heard someone calling my name.

"Kensington!" I looked up, and Teagon was racing toward me, arms outstretched.

"What are you doing here?"

"I've come to collect you," she whispered.

"You have?"

"Yes." She looked over my shoulder. "Can we lose Lurch?"

"Oh, that's Thomas." I turned to him. "Thank you so very much for delivering me safely." I took my bag and pressed the folded money into his hand. "Buy your wife something nice with it."

He left, and I tucked my arm in Teagon's. "Okay, explain, missy."

"I've a heli pilot's license."

"You don't!"

"I do, as a matter of fact."

"How do you know Cortez DeLéon?"

She leaned in close. "I used to work with him," she whispered.

"SIS?"

She nodded and put her finger in front of her lips.

"I can't believe you can fly a helicopter," I said as she helped me buckle up and handed me a headset.

"I've had my license several months now. You have to fly a million hours to get one, so don't worry, you're safe with me."

I smiled. "I didn't doubt it."

Once in the air, I asked her where she was taking me.

"Teterboro."

"And from there?"

Her playful demeanor turned serious. "I'll be returning to London with you, Kenz."

"As?"

"Security."

"Is it really necessary?"

"DeLéon will fill you in once he arrives."

"We're traveling to London with Cortez?"

"I thought you knew."

"You said you used to work with him. Have you left MI6?"

"No, he did."

"I don't understand."

"Rile, as he's known within the ranks of SIS, resigned a few months ago and formed a private firm. I still work for SIS, but was brought in by my boss to assist with your detail, given my relationship with you."

"Detail?"

"As I said before, security. Same thing, Kenz."

"Do you work for him, then?"

"If by him, you mean Rile, not really. Although when we were both with MI6, he outranked me by quite a bit."

"I'm confused. Did the Queen hire him?"

"What do you think, Kensington?"

"That is what I'd suspected initially."

When she didn't say anything more, I looked out at the island of Manhattan below us, thinking how I used to love spending time in New York City. The few trips I made into town while staying with Kiki had been disappointing. Even visiting the Whitney, my favorite museum in the world, left me feeling uninspired. The first real excitement I'd felt since I arrived at my mother's compound was when I heard Cortez's voice an hour ago.

Once back in London, I was sure I'd forget all about him, especially with Teagon around. "I've missed you," I said, looking over at her.

"Me too."

She landed the helicopter seemingly with ease and helped me get out of the complicated harness system.

"I'm afraid we have some time to kill." Teagon was chewing the inside of her cheek. "But Rile insisted I get you here as quickly as possible."

I raised a brow at her use of the name; she appeared to be intimidated by the idea of him. "Explain to me again, do you work for him?"

"Not officially, but this is his mission. You could say I'm on loan to his firm."

"Mission? I'm a mission?"

"It's a figure of speech."

"Did he say we couldn't leave?"

"No, but…"

"How long before his flight lands?"

"Another three hours, at least."

"What do you say we head over to Buvette?"

"That would be bloody brilliant. I haven't been since we were last in Paris."

Two hours, thirty minutes, five texts, and three unanswered phone calls from my irate mother later, we were back at Teterboro Airport, waiting for the arrival of Cortez's plane.

"Are you okay?" Teagon asked.

"You mean because of Kiki?"

"Has she given up?"

I looked at my phone. "No, but she has gone from 'where the fuck are you' to 'you've embarrassed me for the last time you ungrateful brat.'"

It didn't matter what my mother said or did; it never had, if I were being honest. I was happier than I'd been in months, and I had Cortez to thank for it. Or was it the Queen I should thank?

Teagon told me over a bottle of Burgundy that her "assignment" with me would last through the new year.

"I've an excuse not to spend the holidays with either of my parents thanks to you."

Not wanting to spend time with our parents was something Teagon and I had in common.

We were on our second glass of wine in the airport lounge—which meant our fourth of the afternoon—when she broached a subject I'd hoped she wouldn't.

"I've noticed that whenever you say 'Cortez,' your cheeks flush."

"They don't."

"Yes. They do. You're hot for him. Don't try lying to me."

"You'll take the piss out of me for his age."

"You always fancy the older ones."

"He's not that old."

"He's not as old as—" She stopped talking and peered over my shoulder.

"He's here, isn't he?"

"I'll just run off to the loo before we board the plane."

I turned around and watched Teagon leave and Cortez walk toward me.

"Kensington."

"Rile."

He smiled. "I see you're pleased with my choice of escort."

"How did you know she's my best mate?"

"I have my sources." He stepped closer, and I breathed in the scent of him.

"I'm sorry I panicked. I suppose I could've gotten myself away from Kiki's, but the idea that Konstantine could arrive at any moment overwhelmed me."

He reached out and cupped my cheek with his palm. "You look well."

"It's been unseasonably warm, so I've been spending time at the pool."

"Not racing speedboats?"

I smiled and felt flush, in part because of the wine, but more because of his closeness. "That too."

"I came to say goodbye that day."

"I know."

"And yet you ran away."

"Cortez, I…" What could I say? I rushed off because I wanted him to kiss me again and I knew he wouldn't?

Or that I wanted to beg him to take me with him instead of leaving me at Kiki's? And that I wanted to be with him more than I wanted to get away from my mother.

Teagon approached slowly, and I waved her over.

"Hello, Rile," she said, bumping his shoulder.

"Good afternoon, Angel."

Angel? He called her angel? And I'd just admitted I was hot for him? Or maybe she'd accused me of it, but either way…oh my God. Cortez and Teagon were together.

She grabbed my arm, probably because I'd gone from flushed to ghostly pale. "It isn't what you think. Angel is my…code name. Work, remember?" She pointed between the two of them. "Rile and Angel."

"I knew that," I lied. Clearly, neither believed me, but at least, they allowed me to save face. "When do we leave?"

"The plane should be fueled and ready whenever you are."

I excused myself and went to the lavatory as much to douse my face with ice-cold water as to use the facilities. Saying I was hot for Cortez was an understatement. Being close to him set my body on fire.

Thinking about our one kiss—the best kiss of my life—made my pulse race.

I couldn't help but wonder if we were traveling in the same plane we'd flown from London and whether I'd be able to lure him back into the stateroom.

When I came out, Teagon was standing outside the doorway, looking at something on her phone.

"Everything okay?"

"What?" she asked, shoving the phone into her bag.

"What's going on?"

"What do you mean?"

"Come on, Teag. I've known you since we were kids. Something is up."

"Otto von Habsburg is in hospital in a coma."

"What happened?"

"Someone tried to kill him."

8

Rile

The reports out of Budapest were sketchy. Some said Otto von Habsburg was dead, others said he was still alive, but on life support. No one was reporting what had happened that left him in either state.

"When did this occur?" I asked Decker, who had been the one to alert me.

"Sometime yesterday."

"Do the authorities have any leads?"

"Only that they believe he knew his assailant."

My every instinct told me Konstantine had something to do with his cousin's attack, but what would his motive be?

"Where are you now?" Decker asked.

"Teterboro Airport, about to leave for London. Teagon Evans and Kensington Whitby are traveling with me."

"Angel?"

"That's right."

"I remember reading in the brief they were friends."

"I've made arrangements with Z for Angel to cover Kensington's detail indefinitely."

"In London?"

"Yes."

He didn't respond.

"Do you have another suggestion?"

"Somewhere more remote."

"You can't be suggesting…"

"She'd be safer there, Rile."

Once on the plane, I excused myself to the stateroom to give Kensington and Angel privacy to talk. Or that's what I told myself.

When I heard the chime indicating we were at cruising altitude, I pulled out the bunk and stretched out on my back. With my hands behind my head, I stared at the ceiling above me, wondering if bringing someone under my protection into my home was a mistake. It certainly wasn't wise.

I'd just let my eyes drift closed when I heard a knock at the door. "Come in."

Kensington stuck her head in. "Hi."

I sat up. "Hi."

"The co-pilot came out a few minutes ago and said we were on our way to Spain, not England."

"That's right."

"Why?"

I motioned for her to come closer, and she sat beside me.

"Angel informed you of the attack on Otto von Habsburg?"

"Yes."

"Where we're going affords more…security."

"Where are we going, Cortez?"

"To my home on the island of Mallorca."

She turned her head away. "I feel like such a bother."

I reached out and put my fingertips on her chin. "Look at me, Kensington." Staring into her amber eyes, I was transfixed. I longed to touch her lips with mine, but I couldn't let myself.

"Your safety is all that matters."

"Who are you protecting me from? Konstantine? I know it was stupid of me to go to Budapest with him. I would never put myself in a position of being alone with him again. It's why I couldn't stay at Kiki's."

"And what if he comes to you in London?"

"Security would keep him away."

"Would they?"

"Of course. It's what they do."

"Would you feel comfortable leaving your home? Going to the market? Out for dinner or to the pub?"

Her eyes bored into mine, questioning. "How long will this last?"

"Until we have a better understanding of what Konstantine is up to."

"I should let you get some rest."

"Kensington."

She smiled. "Yes?"

"I wish I were younger."

"I don't." She kissed my cheek, stood, and walked out.

Ten hours later, my plane landed at the small airport on the island of Mallorca, where Kensington and Teagon would be spending the holidays.

I had the valet bring the Range Rover to the airfield, and on the way to the other side of the island, I showed Kensington and Angel around Palma, pointing out the Christmas markets in Puerto Portals and Plaça Major.

"Most of the locals have a bigger celebration on *Fiesta de los Reyes* or the Three Kings Festival than they do on Christmas, but you'll find holiday events all over Mallorca. Perhaps tomorrow night we'll come back into town and see the light and ice festival and have dinner." I looked over at Kensington as she took it all in. "Is this your first time on Mallorca?"

"I was trying to remember the last time I was in Spain. It's been years."

"In Madrid, yes?"

"I was nine or ten. A girl."

A child. And I'd been a man of twenty. The idea of it reinforced what I'd said earlier when I told her I wished I were younger.

I peered in the rearview and caught Angel studying me. Our eyes met and she smiled. It was unusual for me that I couldn't get any kind of read on what she was thinking.

"Here we are," I said, pulling into the drive that would take us through the acres of oak forest, past the olive terraces, two guest houses, and finally, to the main residence. To access the small chapel and cemetery and the winery that hadn't been used in several decades, one would have to travel farther north, beyond the house.

When the property I now owned came up for sale, I'd purchased it immediately. The historic estate sat on over two-hundred acres and had direct access to the sea along with spectacular views of the entire Bay of Palma.

The main house had four floors plus a solarium on the roof, all easily accessed by a lift and completely renovated before my purchase. Each level above the lowest had decks or terraces that stretched the entire width of the structure.

The pool area and the trail that led down to the sea, along with terraced gardens with fountains and waterfalls, were on the lowest level. There was also an indoor-outdoor kitchen and barbecue, two changing rooms each with a full bath and shower, a wine cellar, laundry, and several storage rooms.

Still on that level, there was a one-bedroom apartment where my housekeeper lived, that had a lounge, kitchen, bedroom, and bathroom.

The next was at driveway-level and had a garage with parking for five vehicles. Here, there was a large workout and game room, an indoor pool and jetted spa, and two combination bathroom-changing rooms bigger than most locker rooms I'd been in.

Above that were the main quarters with an expansive living room, a gourmet kitchen with a walk-in pantry, an office, two bathrooms, and two dining areas—one formal and one informal.

Four bedrooms were on the next level. Two had bathrooms en suite along with a shared lounge and dual dressing rooms. The other two bedrooms were smaller and shared a bathroom.

On the fifth floor, there was the solarium with an infinity pool and kitchen and two bathrooms. At the far end, I'd added another master suite with a dressing room, full bath and shower, a double-sided fireplace, and windows that rolled into the ceiling above, giving the bedroom area open access to the view of the bay. It's where I slept every night I was home.

While the house was far too large for me to live in alone, I did, and the thought of sharing it with anyone rankled. It would be better if Kensington and Angel stayed in one or both of the guest houses. However, the reason they were with me at all was for Kensington's safety. Could I ensure it if she wasn't living in the main residence? Not as easily.

Instead, I'd let them stay in the suites on the fourth floor since I slept on the solarium level anyway.

"This is your home or your family's?" Angel asked from the back seat.

"Mine alone," I murmured, looking at Kensington.

Her mother's compound was more stately than this, and I doubted her father's was anything less. Kensington had inherited her residence in London from her grandparents, and it too was imposing.

"This is brilliant," she murmured, gasping when we came out of the oak canopy and could see the bay.

I'd never cared about another's opinion of my home. It was mine. With Kensington, her praise made my chest puff out.

"We can take a walk down to the beach later, if you'd like." Angel could come along, of course, but something inside me hoped she wouldn't.

I took their bags in and showed them to the fourth floor.

"Where do you sleep?" Kensington asked when I showed her into the master bedroom and Angel to the companion suite.

"On the level above."

"But your things are in here." She pointed to the open door of the dressing room.

"My apologies. I'll move them before you retire for the night."

"That isn't what I mean, Cortez. I don't want you to give up your bedroom for me."

I smiled and walked over to the windows. "You aren't."

Her forehead scrunched.

"I promise. Would you like to get settled now?"

"I'd rather you show me around, if you don't mind."

"You two go ahead," Angel said, coming to the bedroom door. "I have some work to catch up on."

We took the lift to the lowest level. Given it was unseasonably warm for December, I invited her to make use of the outdoor pool.

"Hello, *Señor* Cortez. Welcome home," I heard Marta, my housekeeper, say. I walked over and embraced the woman I'd known since I was a teenager.

"Kensington, meet Marta. Should you need anything and I'm not available, Marta will help you find it." I went on to explain that another guest was getting settled on the fourth floor and both women would be staying with me indefinitely.

I'd already made arrangements for additional household help. Since my parents would be spending the holidays in Madrid, the staff from their Mallorca residence would be available to assist Marta when needed.

Kensington commented favorably on each level of my home, but it was the solarium that she fell in love with, as had I.

"It's breathtaking," she said, marveling at the one-hundred-and-eighty-degree views. "What is that over there?" She pointed toward the chapel.

"Many of the historic properties on the island have private chapels."

"Is that a cemetery?"

I nodded, not wanting to encourage questions about that particular part of the estate.

"This is where I sleep," I said, showing her the place I considered my sanctuary.

"Oh. I see." She smiled when I hit the switch that rolled up the floor-to-ceiling windows. "No wonder you don't sleep below."

I kept the fireplace cleaned and stacked with new wood, so I knelt down and lit it while Kensington peeked into the bathroom.

"You have the same layout," I said when I saw her standing by the jetted tub.

"Does this open as well?" she asked.

I hit a switch, and instead of rolling into the ceiling, the window above the bath split in the middle and tucked into pockets in the walls on either side.

"No luxury spared," she murmured.

"She belongs here," said the woman who too often of late interrupted my thoughts.

I closed my eyes and rested my hand on the fireplace's mantel. *Stop it.*

"Let go, Cort. Stop fighting. Let her into your heart."

"Come," I said to Kensington, rushing her out of my space and over to the lift. "Please make yourself at home. There are intercoms you may use to contact Marta if there's anything you need."

"Would you still like to take a walk down to the beach later?" she asked.

I shook my head. "You and Angel may go. There's much work I need to catch up on, given my unplanned trip to New York."

I saw the flash of hurt in her eyes but made no apology. If anything, Celestina's words only reminded me of my resolve to stifle any feelings I'd developed for Kensington.

I walked back to my sleeping quarters and stretched out on the bed.

"Shame on you," came the voice I chose to ignore.

Twenty minutes later, as I stood against the railing, looking out at the sea, Kensington and Angel walked out to the pool five floors below me.

The hot-pink bikini she wore, similar to the one I'd seen in photos, was in stark contrast to the blue water of the pool. She dove in and swam underwater to the opposite end. I continued watching as she and Angel made several more laps before Kensington climbed out, removed her bikini top, and stretched out her fuck-ing perfect half-naked body on a chaise.

I couldn't look away. I had to look away. Every time I did look away, my eyes were drawn back to her. Every part of me wanted to touch every part of her. Was it so wrong?

I turned my head to the right and looked down at the cemetery where my beloved Celestina rested. Seeing the headstone, even from a distance, reminded me that wanting Kensington wasn't just wrong, being with her was out of the question. That part of my life was finished. I'd loved once and lost everything. I'd not do it again.

I walked back into the bedroom and pulled out the book I'd started in Budapest. Later, I'd let Marta know I'd have dinner in my suite, and tomorrow, I'd leave for Madrid to spend Christmas with my family.

Kensington wasn't here for a holiday, she was here because she needed protection. I knew enough about her life that I'd contacted Z and asked specifically for Angel to be put on her detail. There was no one else Kensington was close to other than her deceased grandparents. I also knew Teagon would have no desire to spend the holidays with her family.

Mallorca was six hours ahead of Naples, Florida. I picked up my mobile, checked the time, and placed a call.

"Rile? Long time no talk," joked Casper.

"Are you interested in an assignment?"

"I thought you'd never ask."

"It will be faster if you fly commercial."

"Not a problem, Rile. Just get me the hell out of here."

I told her I'd email her flight confirmation as soon as I booked it.

Casper had suffered a loss like I had, although hers was more recent. Her husband had been killed in an op a little over a year ago. With no other family, I knew she'd be the first to take on a job over the holidays. I could tell myself that her being a woman had no influence on my decision to contact her over another independent, but I'd be lying.

While I couldn't allow myself to pursue Kensington, I wasn't ready to watch any other man do so either.

9

Kensington

"What's wrong?" Teagon asked when I pushed my way into her room and flopped down on the bed.

"It's almost as if there's a voice inside his head, and the minute he gets close to kissing me, it tells him to stop. And not just stop, to push me away."

"Pretty nice digs, though." She stood and walked out to the terrace. "It's so beautiful here."

"Right?"

"Think it's warm enough for a swim?" she asked.

"Outside, you mean?"

"Is there another option?"

I told her that in addition to the pool on the lowest level—the one we were looking at—there was another on the top floor, plus an indoor pool somewhere. This place was so big, I couldn't remember where I'd seen it.

"Rile said he slept above us. Where the pool is?"

I nodded. "You should see it." Actually, I didn't want her to. I pictured him there, naked naturally, because a man like Cortez would surely sleep that way.

"So that one?" she pointed below us.

"I'm game, as long as it's heated."

"Wuss."

I changed into my suit but left everything else in my bag. There'd be time to unpack later. I grabbed a cover-up and met Teagon by the lift.

"I feel like we're back to being schoolmates."

"Gawd, but we got in a heap of trouble then," she said, shaking her head.

"Wasn't that long ago." I winked.

"Oh, boy." Teagon laughed and rolled her eyes. "And I'm supposed to be protecting you."

"About that…you don't think it's a bit over the top?"

She shook her head, and all evidence of amusement washed from her face. "Konstantine is dangerous, Kenzie. Don't doubt it."

When I rolled my eyes, she put her hand on my arm.

"I'm here to protect you, not to be your best mate. You need to remember that I'm working."

The pool was heated, and the swim felt bloody fantastic—especially after Teagon's scolding. I did a few laps, climbed out, and saw that Marta had left a stack of towels near the chaises. I spread one out and removed my bikini top, anxious for the sun to bake the stress toxins out of me.

A few minutes later, Teagon sat beside me. "You're teasing the tiger, all right."

"You can't be serious."

She laughed. "I'd love to see the look on Rile's face right now. He's probably swallowed his tongue."

I shielded my eyes from the sun. "He's European, Teag. Topless sunbathing isn't exactly rare."

"Your tits are so much nicer than mine."

"Sod off."

"I'm serious. I'm leaving my top on."

I flipped onto my stomach and turned my head so I could see the upper levels of the house. Cortez was leaning on the railing of the top floor, and even from here, I could tell he didn't look happy. He could bloody well sod off too. If he didn't want me around, he had plenty of options. Like letting me go home, for example.

I turned away, and when I looked back, he was gone.

"What's Cortez's deal, anyway?"

Teagon sighed and rolled to her stomach. "I've heard rumors."

I faced her and propped my head on my hand. "Share."

"It's been some time, but evidently, he was involved with a woman who was killed. Some kind of accident."

"Seriously?"

"Remember I said rumor."

"I guess that would explain why he's so standoffish. At least in part. How long ago did you say?"

"I've no idea. It's all very hush-hush."

"Why?"

Teagon shrugged. "It's just that way in the intelligence world with our own. No matter who it is."

"He kissed me once."

She raised her eyebrows.

"Best bloody kiss of my life."

"Figures."

"Who was the best kiss of your life?"

Teagon shook her head and laughed. "Oh no, we're not going down that road."

"Why not?"

"I've bleached it from memory."

"Your best kiss? That makes no sense. Why wouldn't you want to remember it?"

"Because I'll never see him again." She looked away.

"What happened to him, Teag?" God, I hoped he hadn't died too.

"He's an American."

"*Well!* That explains everything."

She turned her head so I could see her eyes, and in them, I saw the same hurt I felt when Cortez pushed me away a few minutes ago.

"What happened?"

"He got back with his ex-girlfriend."

"The wanker! While you were involved?"

"Yes. Involved is a good word."

"How'd you meet this American?"

"He was my flight instructor."

"Gordon Bennett!"

"Can we change the subject now?" Teagon sat up and pointed behind me.

"What?" I turned my head and saw Cortez walking in the opposite direction of the house. "Where's he going?"

Teagon shrugged.

"I'm going to change," I said a few minutes later, standing and grabbing my bikini top and cover-up.

"Liar. You're going to spy."

Without answering, I rushed over to the lift and took it to the fourth floor. From there, I could see

Cortez clearly as he knelt by a gravestone in the small cemetery.

I gave up watching after a while, only getting up every so often to see if he was still there. He was, long after the sun went down, long after Marta made dinner for Teagon and me.

"Is he okay?" I asked, thinking it was my friend standing behind me.

"Sí," said Marta, startling me when she put her hand on my shoulder. "He goes to talk to her every night when he is here."

"Who was she?"

"Celestina. His wife. Beside her, rests their unborn child."

I gasped and covered my mouth; I wrapped my other arm around my stomach.

I thought about how Cortez had come to comfort me the night he and Grinder saved me from Konstantine, and again on the plane when I couldn't sleep. I wished I could go to him, ease his sorrow the way he had my fear. I knew better than to try. While I welcomed him in my life, he pushed me out of his.

It wasn't until the next night at dinner that Marta reported Cortez had left before sunrise.

"Where did he go?" I asked.

"To spend Christmas in Madrid with his family."

"What the hell?" I mouthed to Teagon, who shrugged and pulled out her mobile when it vibrated.

"There's another person from his team arriving in the morning. She'll be staying on here as well."

"*She?* Who is she?"

"Casper."

I raised a brow.

"I haven't worked with her, but I know of her. She was a really good agent."

"Was?"

"She still is, but retired from the CIA. Quit is more accurate."

"Do you know why?"

Teagon nodded. "Her husband was killed in an op. Rumor is the agency covered up his cause of death."

"Why is she staying on?"

"Added layer of protection."

Because Cortez wasn't here and wouldn't be. Gone were his promises of taking us into town to see the

Christmas lights or visit the markets. Without a word, he'd fled to Madrid, solely to get away from me.

The next morning, I took the lift down one level, wondering if there were stairs somewhere. Surely there had to be. What if the lift broke?

"Oh! Good morning," I said to a woman standing in the kitchen who, even from the back, looked nothing like Marta.

"Good morning," she responded, turning around to look me up and down. "Kensington?"

"That's right. Casper?" I stepped forward and held out my hand. "Good God," I groaned when she shook it. "I thought you were supposed to protect me, not break me."

She laughed. "Sorry about that."

"Hey," I heard Teagon say, coming in from outside.

"Wait. How did you get down here?"

She pointed behind her. "The stairs?"

"What stairs?" I walked outside, and sure enough, there was an outdoor stairwell. Not quite sure how I'd missed it. Well, I knew how I'd missed it; my mind was clouded with lust. No more, though. Even if Cortez were here, I swore off him last night. What kind of arsehole leaves on holiday without saying as much as happy Christmas?

When I came back inside, Teagon and Casper were in the midst of something, but immediately stopped talking.

I walked over to the dining table and took a handful of grapes from the bowl of fresh fruit. "If it's about me, say it when I can hear you."

Casper looked from me to Teagon, who took a deep breath.

"That isn't always a good idea."

I pulled out a chair, sat down, and rested my elbows on the table after I grabbed a banana. "Why not?"

"There are things we should be aware of that you shouldn't," Casper answered.

I thought that over. "Because I'd react and you wouldn't?"

"Precisely," said Teagon. "All you need to know is that Casper and I will work in shifts. One of us will be with you and/or watching you at all times."

Casper leaned forward. "Do you understand?"

"So dramatic," I muttered under my breath.

Both women glared at me.

"You know, the two of you could star in a BBC show about spies. Seriously, just look at you."

Teagon had long, curly, dark blonde hair and blue eyes and looked like a girly-girl, although I knew she was anything but. I'd seen her take down both of her brothers, and they were twice her size.

Casper had shoulder-length, straight, dark almost-black hair that was shaved on the side and green eyes. I already knew her strength, given she almost broke the bones in my hand, but looking at her, I knew she could snap my neck without breaking a sweat. I shuddered.

Teagon rolled her eyes. "Might defeat the purpose of being spies."

"Do all of you have tattoos?" I asked Casper, checking out the detail of her sleeve.

"All of who?"

"You know, Cortez, Grinder, you."

She thought about it for a minute. "Pretty much everyone with the Invincibles does."

"Lynx doesn't," said Teagon.

"Who's Lynx?"

"MI6," they answered at the same time.

"Well, not anymore," Teagon added.

I had no idea what they were talking about, but I wasn't interested in an explanation. "So, what happens now?"

"What do you mean?"

"You know, can we go into town, have lunch or something?"

Again, Casper looked from me to Teagon, who shrugged.

"Rile was going to take you, so I guess we can," said the woman who had been my best friend for years.

"That isn't what he told me," said Casper.

I could feel the muscles in my shoulders tightening. "I would love to hear what he told you, since he didn't tell me a bloody thing."

10

Rile

I felt the muscles in my shoulders tightening and brushed my lower lip with my finger. Kensington was angry.

"What is it, Cortez?" my mother asked, joining me in the sitting room.

"Trouble on Mallorca, I fear."

"Hmm."

"Say it, Duchess."

She stood and walked out to the Christmas tree that was tall enough to reach the second landing of the vestibule.

I followed. "Mother?"

"Why are you here, Cortez, instead of there?"

"I answered that question two days ago when I arrived."

"Remember this?" she asked, taking an ornament from the tree. "You made this when you were in year one."

I remembered it well. There were many things I recalled from that year, including my first premonition.

"You came racing into the room, insisting that there was something amiss in the garage," said my mother, reading my thoughts. "Your father couldn't get past the notion that you'd been out there in your pajamas, but I knew straight away."

"You told him to check, and when he heard it from you, he raced outside."

"One of the chauffeurs was pinned beneath a car. He'd been changing a flat and the jack slipped. You saved his life that night. That's when I knew."

To this day, my sixth sense, ESP, clairvoyance, whatever one preferred calling it, was often as much of a curse as a blessing. When I was younger, the second sight, as my mother referred to it, often resulted in debilitating migraines that could last for days.

"Why are you fighting so hard against this, Cortez?"

I left my mother by the tree and walked over to where I knew my father kept the brandy. I poured myself three fingers and downed it.

When she came and stood in front of me, my eyes bored into hers. "You know why."

"Glare at me all you want. You don't intimidate me."

I never had, because my mother had the ability to look straight into my soul and know exactly what I was thinking and feeling. What angered me was that, even knowing, she'd asked why.

"She wouldn't—"

"Don't," I spat. "You may know me, but you don't know what she would or wouldn't want." I poured another glass and drank it down.

She rested her hand on my arm. "She wouldn't want you to stop living, Cortez, and that's what you've done."

I closed my eyes against the pain that settled in my head and in my heart. I could feel Celestina, but she didn't speak. She didn't need to.

"Go home, Cortez."

"I'll leave after Christmas. That's two days."

"Go home today. Now."

When I shook my head, my mother leaned forward and kissed my cheek.

Later, at dinner, I gave my parents the gifts I'd planned for them to open on Christmas Eve and told them I'd left those for my brother and his family beneath the tree. When I stood, my father did too and embraced me before my mother walked me to the door where my bag already sat.

"Happy Christmas, Cortez."

"Happy Christmas, Duchess."

It was midnight when I approached the gates of my home. I stopped the car and pulled out my mobile.

"I'm here," I said when Angel answered.

"I know," she responded, yawning. "I've just watched you pull up to the gate."

"You're awake."

"You'd see to it Z would have my job if I weren't."

I laughed.

"I'm glad you're back, Rile."

"How is she?"

"You'll see."

I pulled into the garage and took the lift straight up to the fifth floor. I could see a glow coming from my suite and thought perhaps Angel had raced up and lit the fire, although that made no sense nor would she have had the time.

I stepped into my bedroom, dropped my bag on the floor, and discovered why there was a roaring fire. Kensington was fast asleep in my bed.

After toeing off my shoes, I padded over, mesmerized by her beauty—awake or asleep. I put my hand on the wall when a sad feeling permeated my chest. It was her pain, and I'd been the cause of it.

I crawled into bed, behind her, powerless not to give her comfort. When I wrapped my arm around her waist, she released a soft sigh and settled her back into my front. Her troubled sleep eased, and slowly, her pain dissipated. She turned her body to mine and nestled her naked form against my clothed one. I raised her chin with my fingertips and softly brushed her lips with mine, startling her awake.

She blinked. "Cortez?"

"Shh. Go back to sleep."

"I'm not dreaming? You're really here?"

"I am."

"You're not angry I'm in your bed?"

"I wondered if perhaps I was the one dreaming." There was only so much resisting I could do. Once again feeling powerless, I put my hand on her neck and brought my mouth to hers.

As our kiss deepened, I trailed my fingertips down her body to her breast and then pulled back to look at her. "You are magnificent," I said before taking her hard nipple between my teeth. With that small bite of pain, Kensington's body writhed. I put my hand on the soft flesh of her bottom and pulled her closer, pressing my hardness against her until she moaned.

I rolled her to her back and pushed her thighs apart. The scent of her arousal engulfed my senses. I leaned forward, unable to resist a taste. She grabbed the back of my shirt when I licked between her folds and thrust a finger into her heat.

"I know I'm dreaming," she whimpered. "Please, God, don't let me wake up."

When I added a second finger and sucked on her sensitive nub, Kensington's back arched as she cried out. I curled the tips of my fingers, sucking harder as she rode out her powerful climax.

"Taste yourself on me," I murmured, bringing my mouth to hers. When I ran my tongue over her lips, they opened.

She pulled back and stared into my eyes as she unfastened the buttons on my shirt. When she reached the bottom button and went for my trousers, I grasped her wrist with my hand.

"Please," she begged.

"Not tonight, Kensington," I murmured. When I tried to kiss her again, she pulled back.

"Why not?"

Could I explain that it was too important to me? That I had to be certain I was ready before joining our bodies together? Would she understand it would mean more to me than casual sex? That it could never be casual between us?

The lines in her forehead softened as did the look in her eyes. "I understand." She rested her hand on my heart. "Can I stay?"

"I won't let you go."

Kensington smiled and rested her head where her hand had been. I could *feel* her understanding, even though I couldn't read her thoughts—and that terrified me more than anything else.

When I woke after sunrise, Kensington was gone. I got out of bed and walked to the window. My heart stopped when I saw her. She was sitting on the grass above Celestina's grave.

11

Kensington

When the sun on the horizon interrupted my dreams, I got out of bed and dressed. I had no intention of walking to the cemetery. No intention of leaving the house. In fact, I'd planned to sit in the solarium and watch the sun come up over the water. Instead, it was as though I was beckoned to come to where I now sat.

I ran my fingers over the letters carved into the stone. "Celestina Martínez DeLéon." My heart clenched when I realized she was my age when she died six years ago. Marta had said that her and Cortez's unborn baby was buried beside her, but the headstone made no mention of an infant.

"Tell me how to ease his pain," I whispered, wishing I could talk to the woman who had been his wife, the mother of his child, whom I knew he'd loved with all his heart. Still loved, immeasurably.

A warm breeze, in contrast to the chill of the early morning, washed over me, and I closed my eyes.

"Love him." A voice inside my head spoke to me.

Being beside him, having his hands on me last night, felt so right. He never answered me when I asked him why we couldn't make love, but it was as though he had. Understanding, like the warm breeze this morning, washed over me. He wasn't ready, but he was also unwilling to let me go.

Today was Christmas Eve. I never would've predicted that Cortez would return until after the holidays. In fact, I remembered him saying that Epiphany was celebrated more in Spain. That's why I slept in his bed. I missed him more than was logical, and by lying between the bedclothes that smelled of him, I felt like he was wrapped around me. I expected there would be more than a week before he'd return, and by then, Marta would've changed his sheets.

When I felt his arms around me, I was so certain it was a dream. I willfully chose not to open my eyes, praying it would go on and on. It was the feeling of his lips on mine that roused me. It felt so real because it was.

I turned my head when I sensed him watching me and then looked back at the stone. I brought my knees to my chest and wrapped my arms around them. I wasn't ready to leave. In fact, I couldn't.

I wondered if this was how Cortez felt when he spent hours sitting beside the place where his wife's body rested, unable to make himself leave.

When I looked again, he was gone.

Since it was too chilly for a swim this morning, I took the trail down to the beach and ran as far as I could before the sand turned into rock.

I was about to run back the way I'd come when I looked up and saw Casper standing on the rocks above me. I shielded my eyes from the sun.

"Do you need something?"

When she shook her head, I felt like flipping her off. "Are you just going to stand there and watch me?"

She walked down the rocks closer to me. "What part of 'it's my job to watch you' don't you understand?"

"It was a bloody walk on the beach."

"Which you're not supposed to do unaccompanied. Let's go," she said, reaching for my arm.

"That isn't necessary," I said, jerking it away from her. "All you have to do is inform me of my boundaries, and I'll respect them. You don't have to get nasty."

When we reached the stairs, Teagon was coming down. "What's wrong?"

"I found her down on the beach—alone."

"Kenz, you can't—"

"I got it," I said, racing past her and up to the fourth floor.

Given I'd been sleeping in Cortez's bed since the night after he left for Madrid, I'd insisted Casper take the master that sat empty. I went into one of the smaller bedrooms, closed the door behind me, and flopped on the bed.

"What part of 'it's my job to watch you' don't you understand?" I mimicked with a scowl. I hated being patronized.

There was a knock I wished I could ignore on the door. I wanted to be alone, but the knock persisted.

"Come in."

The handle jiggled. "It's locked."

Since it was Teagon's voice on the other side, I stood and let her in.

"Are you okay?" she asked, stepping in and closing it again behind her.

"As I said to her, it was a bloody walk on the beach."

She nodded. "If you want to know the truth, I think she was angry that you slipped past her. Rile would be furious with her if he knew."

"She doesn't need to be such a bitch."

"I know this is difficult, Kenzie, really I do."

"Why is she still here? We didn't need her here before. Is Cortez planning to leave again?"

"I can't answer that. Casper works for Rile—err, Cortez."

"I was in his bed when he arrived last night."

"What happened?"

"He didn't ask me to leave."

She sat down on the small bed, and I sat beside her. "It's just so confusing."

"Believe me," she sighed. "I understand."

"It's almost as though I can feel him. Does that make any sense?"

Teagon looked away.

"What?"

"There are rumors."

"Here we go with the rumors again. What now?"

"Some say that Rile is psychic."

"You're joking, and it isn't funny."

My friend put her hand on my arm. "I'm not joking. I've heard stories about his mum too."

"What of his mum?"

"You've heard of the Cambridge Five, yes?"

"Who hasn't if they've gone to school in the UK?"

"Rile's mother worked for SIS. It's said she was the one who exposed the final two. Up until she did, it was the Cambridge Three."

I cocked my head. At the very least, this ridiculous tale had gotten my mind off my sexual frustration, even if only for a few minutes. "Are you saying she read their minds and found they were Russian spies?"

"I don't know how she did it but, essentially, yes."

I stared at her long enough that if she'd been joking, she wouldn't have been able to maintain a straight face.

"Something happened last night," I said.

"What? Did he read your mind?"

"The other way around."

"You read his?"

"I can't explain it. We were…fooling around—"

"You were?"

"Do you want to hear this?"

"Sorry. Go on."

"I wanted to have sex, but he stopped things."

"And?"

"Like I said, it was as though I could read what he felt. That he was conflicted. He wanted it too, but he stopped himself. I didn't think he was rejecting me. It was more that it was too important to him for us to just have 'sex.'"

"I remember when we were fifteen, and we were at your grandparents' flat in London, and I was on the phone with my boyfriend."

"Tony?"

"Yes! Do you remember what happened?"

"Vaguely. Go on."

"I'd invited him and his best mate over because your grands were out of town."

I gasped. I did remember. "I told you to call Tony back and tell him not to come, because I thought they might come home early."

"I thought you were just being a spoiler, but then no more than twenty minutes later, in they came. I was certain they'd already alerted you that they were on their way, but you were stunned enough that I realized they hadn't."

I knew exactly what she was talking about. It had really thrown me.

"Wasn't the only time either. There were other instances of when you knew things that I didn't remember telling you."

"You're exaggerating."

"That's the thing, Kenz. I'm not."

"That doesn't mean I'm psychic, or that Rile is. Maybe it just means we're intuitive. You've never been hard to read."

"No? You're the only person who knows me who says that."

"Because I know you better than anyone."

She pulled out her phone when it vibrated. "Gotta go. No going outside alone until I get back. Err, I mean, no going outside alone at all."

I rolled my eyes at the lunacy of their overreaction, but I stayed put anyway.

After an hour, I was bored out of my wits. Teagon said not to go outside, she didn't say not to roam the house. However, rather than face another lecture, I told her that I was headed down to the gym. "Do I need to alert Casper as well?"

"She's on outdoor-duty presently."

"Do you need to come with me?"

"Go ahead. There are security cameras—"

I grabbed the door jamb, and my eyes opened wide.

"Don't worry, they aren't in the loo or anything like that."

"Bedrooms?"

"Not in them, but any entries or exits are monitored."

I changed my clothes and went to the lift, wishing it had a list of what was on each floor, like a hotel did, since I couldn't remember where the gym was. I knew it wasn't on the lowest level and doubted it was on the one below this one since that seemed to be all common spaces like the sitting and dining rooms.

I pressed the button for floor two, and when the lift door opened, I knew I was in the right place. I came around the corner and saw Cortez on the treadmill, with his back to me. Our eyes met in the mirror, and I turned around to leave.

"Wait."

I stopped but didn't look back at him. He must find me such an intrusion.

"Don't go."

"I'll come back later and let you finish your run in peace."

He came around and stood in front of me. "Please stay."

"I was just going to run."

"I'm finished. Go ahead."

I tilted my head. "No, you're not. You've just started." His eyes opened wide, but he appeared unperturbed.

"I cannot lie to you, can I?"

I looked away, unable to process the way I was feeling. My conversation with Teagon, and now this. I took a deep breath, let it out slowly, and looked over at the pool. "I'll go for a swim instead."

"In your bikini?"

"Would you prefer in the nude? Sorry to disappoint either way, but I've got a workout suit."

"Very well." He winked.

He went back to the treadmill, and I slipped into the loo to change. When I came back out to the pool, he was gone. I shook my head, donned my goggles, and dove in. I swam the length and back under water, and then did a few freestyle laps. There truly was no better exercise than swimming.

I caught my breath and went for a second round. Midway down the pool, I heard a splash. I glanced behind me and saw Cortez.

He sped past me and then met me again before I completed the lap. I stopped at the far end of the pool and watched him.

He glided through the water like someone who swam competitively. When he transitioned from free to butterfly, I nearly choked. His upper body came out of the water so fluidly and then crashed back in with nary a splash.

"You're a flyer," I said when he stopped at the wall beside me. "A good one."

He scrubbed the water from his face with his hand and laughed. "I'm feeling my age from it."

I removed my goggles. "Trying to show off?"

"Yes." The heat of his gaze was too much. I pushed off the wall and swam to the other end, but he beat me there.

"You're in really good shape."

"Part of the job."

I smiled and shook my head. I dunked into the water and tightened the band on my hair. I hated wearing swim caps, but without one, I had to put my unruly mess in a tight bun.

"I saw you this morning," he said, no longer looking at me.

"I know."

"Why were you there?"

I turned around, pushed off the wall with my feet, and floated on my back.

"Kensington?"

I folded my body in half and put my feet on the bottom of the pool, swishing the water back and forth with my hands.

His eyes met mine. "She was your age when she died."

"Yes."

He put his hands on the pool's deck and climbed out of the water with nothing more than his upper-body strength, and left without another word.

I couldn't help myself from watching the way his tight, firm ass, covered in only a Speedo, moved when he walked. Nor could I help wishing he'd turn around so I could see the front of him.

12

Rile

After my swim, I went in search of sustenance.

I'd given Marta two days off—more that I forbid her to work—but expected she'd left plenty to eat. I wouldn't cast her out of her home, but I wanted her to spend time with her family.

When I walked into the kitchen, Casper was sitting at the table.

"Taking a break?" this is Rile.

"She's upstairs with Teagon."

I opened the refrigerator and found that Marta had it well-stocked. While I'd planned to take Kensington into the village for a special Christmas Eve dinner, we would not go hungry otherwise in my housekeeper's absence.

Sensing Casper wanted to be on her own, I excused myself and rang Decker. "Sorry for the intrusion on a holiday."

"Don't be. I was getting ready to call you."

"About?"

"Konstantine is on the move."

"Where is he now?"

"He's scheduled to fly from JFK to Budapest in a little over an hour. We tracked him from the mother's residence straight there."

"Who do you have on him?"

"Smoke. Once they land in Hungary, Siren will join him."

"Siren? Has she left IMI?" I hadn't anticipated her retirement from Irish Military Intelligence this soon.

"Made her an offer she couldn't refuse."

"Excellent," I murmured. "Many thanks."

"Doin' my job, Rile. Merry Christmas."

I wished him the same and rang off. Things were moving forward quite well for the Invincibles, and I was pleased. The two independent operatives Decker put on this assignment had been near the top of my list of recruits, but I'd never expected they'd come on board before sometime next year.

I showered and shaved but, since I hadn't mentioned dinner to Kensington, put on casual clothes. When I came out of my bedroom, I found her sitting on a bench, looking out at the Balearic Sea.

"I was on my way to look for you." When she turned toward me, her natural beauty took my breath away, as it always did.

"Your eyes are the color of the sea," she said when I sat down beside her. "Why were you looking for me?"

"I wanted to invite you to join me for dinner tonight."

"Just me?"

I nodded.

"What about Teagon and Casper? Is that her name? Casper?"

"Her name is Calla, and dinner would just be you and me."

"On Christmas Eve? I'd hate to go without them. Teagon, at least."

I smiled. "We wouldn't be going without them. They'd be with us, but they'd also be working."

"Right. I forgot. It's their job to watch me." She rolled her eyes, which made me laugh.

"It is, Kensington. Now, what about dinner? Will you join me?"

"I would like that."

"Good." I looked at my watch. "We'll leave in an hour. Will that suffice?"

"Attire?"

"Festive."

I was standing by the trail that led down to the beach when Kensington came outside. The sun was just setting, and in its glow, I couldn't imagine anyone ever being more beautiful. She wore a simple black dress and a dark red, beaded, rope-length necklace. When she approached, I touched the strand with my fingertip. "Garnets?"

"My birthstone."

"Ah, yes, you have a birthday soon, don't you?"

"Next month."

"The fifteenth." I held out my arm. "Shall we?"

She looked over her shoulder. "Where are…"

"Close by."

I'd had two reasons for paying the owner of the small bistro to close for me tonight. The first was for Kensington's safety; the second was that I wanted her all to myself without any distractions.

"It smells fantastic," she said when we walked in.

"*Señor* DeLeón, *bienvenido.*"

I shook the man's hand. "Ponce, please, call me Cortez, and may I present Miss Kensington Whitby."

When she extended her hand, he kissed the back of it. *"Bienvenida,"* he repeated.

"Thank you. It's a pleasure to meet you."

"Please, follow me."

He showed us to the lone table in the center of the room, illuminated both by candles and the lights on the Christmas tree.

I recognized his son, PJ—Ponce Junior—when he brought the bottle of wine I'd chosen to the table, followed by a simple appetizer of Manchego cheese, olives, and chorizo with fresh, warm bread.

"Por La Noche Buena," I said, raising my glass.

"Happy Christmas Eve," she replied so sweetly.

PJ brought our next course of *Escudella*—the rich, traditional soup made from pasta, white beans, and winter vegetables—and we chatted about Christmases she spent with her grandparents at the Queen's country estate in Norfolk.

"What about your parents? You haven't mentioned either of them."

"Once they divorced and Kiki tried her best to take my father for everything he was worth, she wasn't welcome. As far as my dad was concerned, I don't remember a Christmas when he was around. Perhaps when I was very little. He travels almost non-stop. When I last spoke to him, he was in Chile."

"When was that?"

"Right before we left London for America."

"I wasn't able to reach him." I hoped she would believe I'd tried.

"He said it was a miracle I did, given he was in the desert where there was no signal."

"Your grandparents loved you very much."

She cocked her head. "They did, but what makes you say that now?"

"Because you are the daughter of people who cared a great deal for you. It is evident in all that you do. All that you are."

"I will take that as a compliment."

"As it was intended."

Our main course consisted of *Cordero Asado*—roast lamb—and my favorite, *Caldereta de Langosta*. The lobster stew originated on Mallorca. As we ate, I told her about Christmas at *Palacio de la Zarzuela* with my aunt and uncle, Queen Isabella and King Ferdinand.

We rested before our dessert arrived; I stood and walked over to the Christmas tree.

"I have a gift for you," I said, handing her the package I'd had delivered here earlier.

She put her hand on her heart. "Cortez, I—"

"Allow me, Kensington. It would bring me great pleasure for you to have this." Her eyes lit up.

She carefully unwrapped the heavy paper and gasped when she saw the image that lay beneath. "Miró's *Petit Univers.*" Kensington looked up at me in awe. "It's one of my favorites."

I watched as she studied the painting, turning her head to take in the vibrant colors. "Miró once said that he tried to apply colors like words that shape poems, like notes that shape music."

Her fingers traced the shapes depicted in the painting without touching it. To me, it represented the woman sitting across from me, her thin form by the sea, with the moon and stars shining on her, and the creatures from the ocean that frolicked with her.

She raised her head suddenly. "Cortez…"

I smiled. "Yes?"

"It can't be."

"It is."

"The original?" Her eyes filled with tears when I nodded. "It's the nicest gift anyone has ever given me." She looked down at the painting and up at me again. "I've nothing for you," she murmured.

Ah, but she had given me so much already. Her smile and the way her eyes met mine. Her laughter in times of uncertainty. Her mouth, her tongue, the nipples that hardened from my gaze alone. Her wetness, and above all, the gift of falling apart from my hands and mouth.

"Cortez," she murmured, her cheeks flush.

I reached across the table and held my hand out. She placed her palm on mine. "Can you feel what I'm thinking, Kensington?"

She lowered her eyes.

"Look at me, sweetheart. Can you?"

"Sometimes."

"Now?"

"I think so."

"Tell me."

"I'm never shy, Cortez. I never have been, but with you…"

"Shall I tell you, then?"

"Please," she murmured.

"I liked having your body next to mine last night. Very much, in fact."

Her eyes closed, and I watched as a shudder coursed through her. I closed my eyes too, remembering her legs spread for me, the taste of her on my lips, my tongue. She squeezed my hand tightly, and I knew she was remembering too.

Our dessert of almond candy and cookies and Spanish crumble cakes arrived along with two glasses of Moscatel. As I sipped the smoky, sweet wine, I knew what I had to do.

I brought her hand to my mouth and kissed her palm. "There is something we must talk about, Kensington."

"Celestina?" she whispered.

I continued to hold her hand, needing the connection as I told her about the day my heart broke.

"I was on a mission in Iraq in advance of the Battle of Mosul, as part of a team made up of allied militias and international forces along with the Iraqi Government." I took a deep breath. It had been a long time since I told anyone this story. In fact, when I last had, I vowed I never would again.

Kensington weaved her fingers with mine.

"We were in the final planning stages of the attack intended to recapture the city from the Islamic State."

She waited patiently while I gathered my thoughts. I looked into her eyes and saw everything I needed to go on.

"I knew the instant it happened. My chest felt as though a grenade had exploded from inside me. A call came in a few minutes later, confirming what I already knew. My beloved wife died…"

Kensington rested her other hand on top of where ours were entwined. "It's okay, Cortez, please don't feel as though you have to say anything more. I am so very sorry for your loss."

"It was an automobile accident here in the village. A car sped out from one of the side streets, ignoring the stop sign, and hit hers. They told me later she died on impact. I already knew."

When I looked back at Kensington's beautiful face, her cheeks were stained with tears. "I'm so sorry," she whispered.

"She was your age when she died. We'd been married two years. We were ready to start a family."

Her grip on my hand tightened as tears streamed down her face.

"Forgive me for ruining—"

She shook her head. "Please don't apologize for anything, Cortez. I beg you."

"Kensington, I…" I shook my head, unable to continue. She had to know, had to understand, that a part of me died that day. I would never be able to be what I was to Celestina to another woman. No woman could replace her.

My eyes remained on the woman who sat across from me as I felt the warmth of a hand on my shoulder.

"Love her, Cortez. You can love her the way you loved me. Let her in."

I shook my head. "We should return to the house."

"Okay," she said, wiping her tears. "Excuse me?"

"Of course," I said, standing to help with her chair. I watched her walk to the ladies' room, her shoulders heaving.

I thanked our host and his son for the wonderful evening they'd allowed us, and rang Angel to let her know we were ready to leave.

When Kensington came out, I put my hand on the small of her back and guided her outside.

Neither of us spoke on the ride to the house. When we walked inside, she turned and faced me.

"Blessed Christmas, Cortez." She kissed my cheek. "I will never forget all that you have given me."

I watched as she got on the lift, but I didn't join her. I poured a glass of brandy and looked out at the moonlight reflected on the sea.

I cannot, my beloved.

"You must, my love. It's time."

13

Kensington

I pressed the button for the fourth floor, and it illuminated. Yet when the lift stopped and the doors opened, I was on the fifth. I walked to where I'd slept beside Cortez last night as though I was in a trance.

I removed my dress and then my underthings, folded them, and put them on the chair. Naked, I walked over to the fireplace and lit it before crawling into his bed.

I wasn't nervous about him finding me here. I knew in my heart that this was where I was supposed to be. I closed my eyes and waited until I felt his presence.

I opened them and saw him standing in the doorway. He was as naked as I, his beautiful body illuminated by the fire's glow. I sat up and held my hand out to him.

He took it and came to lie beside me. "Kensington," he murmured. "You are in my bed."

He was smiling so I did too. "It seemed the lift had a mind of its own."

The chill that had been in the room was gone. Between the warmth from the fire and the intense heat between our bodies, I felt covered in a sheen of dew. I threw off the bedclothes and trailed my fingertips down from Cortez's lips to his neck, the center of his sternum, to where the trail of salt-and-pepper hair led to his hardness.

He sucked in a breath when I wrapped my hand around his girth. He grabbed my face and held me still while his mouth ravaged mine, and I continued stroking him.

The vibrations from his moans spread from my mouth to my nipples and then my clit. I licked my lips as I imagined licking my way down the trail my fingers had journeyed.

Cortez moved my hand from his cock to his hip, making me pout, but the hunger etched on his face ignited my longing into a fast-burning flame. "Please," I whispered.

"Say it again. Louder."

"Please, Cortez."

He ran his hand down my body like I had his, searing my skin wherever he touched. His focus stayed on my pebbled nipples. When he finally moved to spread my legs open, I couldn't stop myself from writhing.

He moved and settled his body between my thighs.

"Tell me what you want, Kensington."

"You. Inside me," I pleaded.

"I do not have protection, my gorgeous girl."

He lowered his mouth and licked through my folds.

"I'm on birth control," I cried, knowing that he could bring me to an orgasm with his mouth and fingers, but I wanted more.

He stopped and stared into my eyes. "I have not been with another woman…"

I cupped his face with my palm. "Nor I a man, without protection."

He moved his body up and caught my tight nipple between his teeth while his hardness rested at my yearning pussy. His push was slow at first.

"Tell me you want me," he demanded.

"I'll die if I don't have you."

"Say my name."

"Cortez, please," I begged, and with it, he thrust inside.

"You are so tight, so warm," he said, stilling as my body grew accustomed to his size. I wrapped my legs around his waist and grabbed his arse, wanting him to move again.

He thrust slowly, teasing me, and rolled his hips in a circular motion. "So wet for me."

I bit my lip as I felt an orgasm hovering, knowing that when it hit, I would dissolve. Cortez thrust harder and put the tip of his finger on my clit.

"Give me your pleasure, Kensington. I want it."

It felt as though steaming liquid coursed through my veins. I was so close.

"Let go, my darling. I've got you."

He covered my mouth with his, swallowing my scream. As I rode out my own climax, I clenched his cock, making him thrust harder. I could feel the groan building in his chest and kissed him harder as he let it out into my mouth like I had with him.

Cortez licked the perspiration from my neck. "I'm not finished with you, Kensington." He put his hand on my left leg and brought it up so it rested on his shoulder. He thrust again, and I almost came just from the change in angle.

"God, Cortez," I moaned, loving his slow movement as he went deeper than I thought possible.

"Look into my eyes. Match your breathing with mine."

I focused on his demand. When his breathing slowed, mine did too.

"Feel how I move inside you, Kensington." He rolled his hips like he had earlier, but this time, it felt so different. It was as though I could feel every ridge of his hard cock.

He brought his finger to my clit and circled it slowly. "Do not come, Kensington. Focus your mind. Enjoy but do not let yourself go."

Soon, he lifted my other leg and held my ankles together with his hand. He changed the direction of the circular motion he made with his hips and punctuated it with a thrust every few seconds.

He changed positions several times. Each, it seemed, resulted in me feeling him in a way I hadn't previously. Our eyes remained locked on one another's, and our breathing stayed in perfect sync.

He was a masterful, tender, giving lover. No one had ever given me the kind of pleasure Cortez did, and I couldn't imagine allowing anyone other than him to touch my body ever again.

He rested his elbows on either side of my face and continued his thrusts, quickening and deepening them as he kissed me.

"Now, my love," he murmured. "Let yourself fly."

This time when I cried out, he did nothing to silence me. My orgasm went on and on. Just as I felt it beginning to slow, he looked so deeply into my eyes, I felt like his whole body was inside of mine. I watched as he came apart like I had. He kissed me again, and it seemed to go on as long as my orgasm had. His tongue moved within my mouth like his cock had in my pussy.

I never wanted to leave this bed, never wanted our bodies to separate. Sustenance be damned. All I needed to live on was Cortez.

When I woke with the sun, his arm was around me, holding me close to him. I'd never felt so relaxed or at peace in my life, and that was all thanks to the beautiful man whose front was nestled to my back.

Even though we'd made love for most of the night, I wasn't sore. I smiled when I felt his lips kiss my neck and down my spine.

"I love these," he said, as he kissed the dimples above my bottom. "And these." He kissed each of my fleshy cheeks. He continued his way down, tickling the backs of my legs with his tongue until he reached the soles of my feet. "*Feliz Navidad,* Kensington."

"Happy Christmas, Cortez."

He flipped me over so I was on my back, and worked his way up my body, spreading my legs when he reached my heated core. I expected him to linger, but he didn't. Instead, he rubbed his chin with his palm. "I am making your beautiful skin turn red."

"I don't care."

He grazed my stomach with the side of his face, and I laughed.

"Come," he said, getting to his feet and holding out his hand. He led me into the en suite bath and turned on the water in the jetted tub. I groaned, already knowing how good the water would feel, pulsing against my muscles.

He stared into my eyes. "I love the sounds you make. I am learning what each means."

"Pleasure, Cortez. Each one means the same."

He helped me into the bath that could comfortably fit us both. "That is not true," he said, nuzzling my neck and making me giggle. Moments later, he pinched my nipple hard and twisted it. I gasped, and my pussy flooded. That counted as pleasure, then, didn't it?

"Come," he repeated, pulling so I sat between his legs, my back resting against his chiseled pecs and rock-hard abs.

"You are in amazing shape," I murmured, resting my hands on his powerful thighs.

He laughed. "For an old man."

"For any man."

"What would you like to do today?"

"Sleep?"

He laughed again. "I will visit the chapel later. Would you like to join me?"

"Very much." My stomach rumbled. "I didn't think I'd ever be hungry again after last night's feast, but I am."

"As am I," he murmured, reaching between my legs. He stroked me and then pushed me away from him. "Stand and straddle me," he said, turning me to face him.

He placed the tip of his cock against my pussy and pulled me down until he was as deep inside me as he could get.

"Make yourself come, Kensington," he said, placing his hands on my breasts. He went completely still as I found my rhythm. I stopped momentarily when the water splashed. "Keep going," he said, closing his eyes in what looked like ecstasy.

I started to move again, even when the water splashed onto the tile floor. His hands fastened on my waist as he inhaled a deep breath. He pushed his hips up, hard, and groaned his release.

I hadn't come, but I didn't care. I'd lost track of how many times I had in the last several hours. Giving him pleasure made me feel powerful, and I wanted more. I sat back and grabbed the body wash, making a lather in my hands. Slowly, I washed him, cupping his scrotum with one hand while I made him hard again with the other. I reached behind me and drained the water from the tub.

"Stand," I demanded.

He smiled, and I knelt before him, showing his cock the love he'd given me.

14

I didn't think I had another orgasm in me. Not this soon after I'd emptied myself into Kensington's body. I was powerless against the magic of her mouth as she licked and sucked me. I weaved my fingers in her hair, holding her still as I felt a surge of power through me.

This woman kneeling before me was magnificent. Our bodies fit together as perfectly as our souls.

Forty-eight hours ago, I would've refused to believe I would open myself up to her. Now, I couldn't imagine not having her in my arms. I pulled her to her feet and kissed her, tasting myself on her tongue. Already, I wanted her again.

Kensington shuddered with a chill. I grabbed a towel from the warming rack and wrapped it around her. I led her to the bed and sat behind her, running my fingers through her hair to get rid of the tangles.

Her stomach rumbled like it had in the bath, and I laughed. "Yes, okay, I must feed you."

She leaned back against me. "I don't want to leave this room."

I didn't either, but if I didn't, I'd be back inside her body within minutes. I pushed her up, stood behind her, put a robe around her shoulders, and grabbed my workout pants and a sweatshirt.

Once in the lift, I surrounded her body and kissed her hard. "A promise for later," I murmured, reaching inside her robe to tweak her nipple. My efforts were rewarded when the scent of her arousal met my nostrils.

The door opened, and I was pleasantly surprised to find the kitchen empty.

"Sit while I make us something to eat."

"I can help."

I shook my head. "Marta left us a feast." I reached for the platter of fresh fruit and set it on the table, close enough for Kensington to reach. I filled a pitcher with water and put two glasses on the table with it.

Rubbing my hands together, I opened the pantry where I knew Marta kept baked items. There were Spanish crumble cakes like we'd had for dessert last night along with several other pastries. I opened the cupboard and took out a large platter, which I then filled.

"What else may I bring you?"

"Tea?"

I hit my head with my palm, and she giggled—the sound was heavenly. "How could I forget tea?"

Once the water was hot, I brought the teapot and cups to the table and then sat beside her, our arms and legs touching. I plucked a strawberry from the platter and brought it to her lips. When she took a bite and then licked my fingers, I made a plan to bring a bowl of fruit up to our room.

Our room. I waited for the feeling of dread I anticipated with a thought such as that, but it didn't come. Instead, the warmth from her body next to mine, blanketed me against my own guilt or recrimination.

I heard the lift leave the floor and then return a few minutes later.

"Happy Christmas," I heard Angel say after the door opened. She sat down at the table and rested her folded arms on it. "By the look of you both, I'd say this is a very happy Christmas, indeed."

Kensington pointed to the end of the table where the Miró painting sat. "Cortez gave me a Christmas gift last night."

"Yeah?" Angel stood, lifted the paper that covered it, and gasped. "A Miró?"

Kensington nodded. "Isn't it brilliant?"

Angel's eyes met mine. "An original?"

I gave a slight nod.

"Wow. I'm impressed, Rile."

"By what?" asked Casper, coming in from the outside stairwell. "Oh, that? I peeked earlier."

"Please join us," I said to the two of them, waving my hand at the table. "There's plenty of food, more where this came from. Casper, you'll find a French press in the cupboard and coffee beside it." I stood and refilled the tea kettle and set it on the stove. "Angel, there is tea."

"You are such a gracious host, err, boss. We aren't exactly your guests," muttered Angel. "Thanks, nonetheless."

"You are very welcome," I said, returning Kensington's smiling gaze.

Her back was to me, but I could feel the sorrow seeping off of Casper. This would be her second Christmas without her beloved husband, and I knew exactly how hard that would be for her. I rested my hand on her shoulder and watched her wipe away a tear.

As much as I wanted to spend the day alone with Kensington, I had another idea that would allow the three women in the room with me to enjoy the holiday a bit more. It would also keep Casper's mind off her sadness, at least a little.

I went back and sat beside Kensington. "Last night, we spoke about Christmas at the *Palacio de la Zarzuela.*"

Her eyes lit up. "Do tell Teagon and Casper about it, Cortez. It sounded enchanting."

"What if I were to show them instead?"

"That would be brilliant," she murmured.

"Are you certain we'd be welcome?" Angel asked.

"More than," I said, knowing exactly my mother's reaction.

As I predicted, the duchess' exclamation of glee could be heard across the room through my mobile.

"Do hurry, Cortez," she said before putting her hand over her mic, most likely to announce our impending visit. "Please plan to stay, darling," she said before we rang off.

I hadn't considered the notion, but being there would allow Angel and Casper some time to relax, considering the security my family already had on staff.

When we arrived at the airfield in Palma, I went inside the private terminal and made arrangements for our transport. Instead of driving to the DeLéon hangar, I drove to the helipad. When we arrived, I looked at Angel in the rearview. "Would you mind terribly?"

She clapped her hands and let out an exclamation of glee similar to my mother's. "Seriously?" she said, eyeing the Bell 429 helicopter that sat waiting.

"Are you rated?"

She nodded, practically salivating.

"Let's go."

"Wow," said Kensington, running her hand over the supple leather once we were inside and seated. "It's almost like a plane."

Angel delivered us safely to the palace's helipad. "Thanks, Rile," she said, looking back over her shoulder one more time before we walked away.

"You'll get to fly it again in a few days' time."

Her eyebrows went up.

"How did you think we'd get back?"

She shrugged and laughed.

The *Palacio de la Zarzuela* was one of nine "official" residences of the Spanish monarchy and certainly not the grandest.

The Royal Palace of Madrid held that title and was the main residence of the rulers of Spain beginning in 1735. It was the largest palace in all of Europe, with 3,418 rooms and 135,000 square meters. Since the deposition of Alfonso XIII in 1931, it had been used solely for official and state functions.

It was constructed after the Spanish War of Succession, which ended the reign of the Habsburg monarchy—from whom the wretch Konstantine descended—and began the Borbón monarchy, from which I descended.

In the two-hundred and fifty years that followed, Spain experienced great turmoil. The monarchy was abolished, reinstated, and abolished again—many times over.

It was Generalissimo Franco who'd restored the monarchy last, when he named Juan Carlos I de Borbón, my grandfather, as his successor in 1947.

Rather than live in the Royal Palace, he chose the far less ostentatious *Palacio de la Zarzuela* as the site of his main residence. It had been built originally as a hunting lodge in the 1630s and suffered extensive damage in the Spanish Civil War in the 1930s. *Abuelo* Juan, as my brother and I called him, had it rebuilt into the compound it was today.

There were several residences on the grounds, including the King and Queen's—known as the Pavilion—as well as that of my parents, which sat virtually next door to one another on the five-thousand-acre grounds. My brother and his wife also lived within the compound but in a slightly more modest residence than that of our parents.

My father, Juan Cortez DeLéon, and his older brother, King Ferdinand, were two years apart in age, had always been close, and remained so now. My father served as the king's confidant and advisor since his coronation.

Thus, our relationship with my aunt and uncle had always been like that of any other family. From the stories she told about spending holidays with her great-aunt, Kensington's relationship with the Queen of England didn't appear much different than mine with the King of Spain.

My mother and father greeted us warmly upon our arrival, both appearing giddy, looking upon Kensington as a woman with whom I was in a relationship and brought home to celebrate Christmas with my family, as opposed to someone under my protection.

My brother, Osvaldo, and his wife, Maya, along with their two sons, Luis and Alfonso, greeted us as well. I was astounded at how much my nephews had grown since the last time I saw them. Then, they'd been toddlers; now, they were little boys with faces full of mischief, just like Osvaldo and I had been.

While Kensington and Angel appeared relaxed with my family, Casper remained tense and rigid. I was at a loss as to what to do to ease her discomfort when I saw my brother's wife, Maya, approach her.

Soon, the two were in an animated conversation while my mother monopolized the other two women.

"She's lovely," said my father, motioning in their direction. "I'm pleased to see the change in you in only a few days' time. Astounded, but happy."

"I am astounded as well, Father."

"There's something about her… Does she remind you of anyone?"

"Only of herself."

My father poured us each a brandy. "Here's to the miracles of the season."

Kensington turned to look for me, and our eyes met. I raised my glass to her, and she smiled.

"Few greater beauties on this earth other than your mother."

"I would agree."

Shortly before I knew dinner would be served, I put my arm around Kensington's waist. I led her around a corner, pushed her against the wall, weaved my fingers in her hair, and kissed her. Her arms were immediately around my neck, pulling me closer. I rested my pelvis against her, and she quietly moaned.

"I've missed you," I whispered, kissing down her neck. When her body began to move against mine, I knew she'd missed me just as much.

"Cortez? Dinner," I heard my mother's voice from the other room.

"Come," I said, kissing the back of her hand. "The sooner we finish dinner, the sooner we can be alone."

As we went back around the corner, I knew we would not be able to rush off by ourselves as I'd momentarily planned, for seated at the table, were my uncle and aunt.

A traditional *Pavo Trufado de Navidad* was served, including turkey stuffed with truffles, a vast assortment of seafood, and an array of desserts similar to what Kensington and I had eaten the evening before.

"We missed you at *esta noche de dormir*," said my aunt.

When I was a boy, the night before Christmas had been my favorite of the year. After the midnight service, *La Misa Del Gallo* or the Mass of the Rooster, it was Spanish tradition to walk through the streets, carrying torches, playing guitars, and beating on tambourines and drums. This went on until sunrise. As the saying went, *"Esta noche es Nochebuena, y no es noche de dormir,"* which meant "Tonight is the good night and it is not meant for sleeping!"

My eyes met Kensington's, and she smiled. We'd celebrated the night not meant for sleeping in our own way.

"My dear," my uncle began, "I fondly remember the first time your grandfather took Juan and I skeet shooting…"

By the end of the story, we were all laughing uproariously and Kensington was adding stories of her own. She was not only beautiful, charming, and intelligent, she fit in as though she'd known my family for years—because she had.

Celestina had never been comfortable with them, even after we were married. Had I suggested we visit Zarzuela for the holidays, she would've begged me to stay on Mallorca. I momentarily closed my eyes. *Forgive me, my love, for disparaging your memory.*

"You have kept me on a pedestal too long, Cort. You've made it so no one could live up to me, and yet this one is much better suited to you."

When my mother cleared her throat, I met her gaze and stood to help with her chair. "Join me, Cortez," she said, leading me from the room.

"Have you heard anything about Habsburg?"

"Konstantine or Otto?"

"Either."

"I have not, Mother."

"Please excuse yourself and check."

I knew better than to ever doubt my mother's intuition. I sent a group text to Decker, Smoke, and Siren, asking for an update.

Smoke responded first. *OVH is awake and ready to talk,* he reported.

Interesting, I thought to myself as I rubbed my lower lip with my finger. Konstantine's cousin was alive and ready to divulge who had tried to kill him—I had no doubt it hadn't been an accident. I was also certain of his assailant. What I didn't know was why Konstantine would want his cousin dead.

After dinner, the entire family, the King and Queen included, left the palace grounds to deliver food and gifts to those less fortunate. Each year, where they went was kept a secret until the very last minute.

I understood the security nightmare posed by this annual event; however, I also knew my uncle. If anyone had suggested to him that he not honor the annual tradition, they would not have liked his response.

I was pleased when our caravan pulled up to the *Hospital Infantil Universitario Niño Jesús*. Armed with gifts for the children in the hospital, their siblings and parents, along with the doctors, nurses, and other hospital staff, we were divided into groups to make our deliveries.

Naturally, Angel and Casper were with Kensington and I. Since we were joined by six members of palace security, they too were able to participate in the fun.

Each time, it was the mother of the ill child whom Kensington immediately gravitated to. I found it interesting, given her relationship with her own mother. But then, her mother hadn't raised Kensington, her grandmother had.

"I received an update regarding Otto von Habsburg. He has come out of his coma," I said to Kensington after we returned to the palace.

"He's alive?" she asked, turning in my arms as we watched the dancing flames in the fireplace of the room my parents chose for us.

I nodded and then brought my lips to hers. "Another Christmas miracle, I suppose."

"Another?"

"My father proclaimed one earlier today upon seeing you and I together."

"Is it a miracle, Cortez?"

"For me, yes, I must say it is. I wasn't sure I was capable of opening up to anyone the way I have to you. And before you begin to feel immense pressure less than a day after we first made love, I credit you with making me see I could open my heart again. I do not expect you to hold it in your hand forever."

"And what if I want to, Cortez? Will you allow me to?"

"Can you honestly say you're ready for that, Kensington?"

She stiffened. "Evidently, you don't believe so."

I brought her fingertips to my lips and kissed them. "What I believe is that we have plenty of time to explore each other's bodies and souls before we hold each other's hearts."

As I watched Kensington's eyes, I felt as though an invisible wall had raised between us. I had no idea what she was thinking, and more, she didn't want me to know.

15

"Will you be staying on to celebrate *Fiesta de los Reyes*?" the Duchess of Soria asked as the two of us sat enjoying morning tea.

"I've no idea," I responded, steeling my thoughts as my gaze met hers.

"Cortez has not said?"

"No, ma'am."

"Odd."

"Perhaps he is unaware of his schedule." I excused myself and walked over to the buffet to plate a pastry and some fruit.

"There she is," I heard him saying, walking up to kiss me. "I thought perhaps you'd join me for a swim."

"Mmm, I should have. Perhaps I'll take a few laps later this morning." He studied me, but like with his mother, I kept my thoughts to myself.

When I turned back to pour more tea, he moved my hair from my neck and kissed my nape. I felt my knees weaken when the stiff tip of his tongue replaced the softness of his lips. I leaned back against him and then remembered we were not alone. However, when I turned my head, his mother was no longer at the dining table.

"You are holding yourself back from me," he said, scrunching his eyes. "You are punishing me, no?"

"No," I answered too quickly. "Don't be ridiculous."

"Two lies. Two punishments, my sweet."

I laughed, but Cortez did not. "Come." He led me over to the staircase and, when we reached the first step, swung me into his arms and carried me the rest of the way up.

He pushed the bedroom door open with his foot and deposited me on the bed.

"I've imagined doing this to you."

"Doing what?"

"Giving you the punishment you deserve."

"You've got to be…" But he wasn't joking. I knew that now. I got off the bed, knelt before him, and rested my hands on his thighs. I looked into his eyes, imploring him. "Please, Cortez," I begged. "Forgive me."

I moved my hands from his thighs to his belt, but before I could unfasten it, he pulled me to my feet, cupped my arse, and kissed me—hard.

He weaved his fingers in my hair and pulled my head back. "You will not hold yourself away from me. Not your body or your thoughts. Do you understand, Kensington?"

I whimpered at the bite of pain when I tried to nod my head.

"If I upset you, you must tell me. If you are unable, then settle your mind and let me in. Let me hear the words you can't bring yourself to say."

"Cortez, I…" I did my best to quiet my mind as he said. *How can you say I'm not ready to take your heart? You're all I've ever wanted.*

"I see. You thought I was rejecting you. Making light of what happened between us?"

I nodded.

He held my throat with his hand and kissed me. *"Never.* Do you understand?"

I couldn't answer; his mouth pressed so hard into mine.

"I felt so far away from you last night and this morning," he said, holding his cheek next to mine. "It was hell."

"For me too."

He hurriedly stripped me of my clothes and pushed me onto the bed before taking his own off.

My pussy clenched, wondering what he planned to do with me, hoping he'd follow through with his threat to punish me, even though I'd begged him not to.

He moved a freestanding mirror between the end of the bed and the fireplace he'd just re-lit.

"On all fours, my sweet. Face the fire." When he winked, I smiled.

He knelt on the bed behind me. "Watch in the mirror, Kensington."

He brought one hand down on my arse. The slap stung, but didn't hurt. He did it again on the other side before thrusting two fingers into my seeping pussy.

"You are so wet," he murmured, bringing his fingers to his lips and sucking my essence from each. When finished, he gave me two more slaps and then thrust the same fingers back inside me. My eyes rolled back in my head as I felt an orgasm looming.

"Watch, Kensington," he demanded. I opened my eyes and met his gaze in the mirror. "Do you think you've been punished enough?"

"No, Cortez."

He grinned and raised his eyebrows. "No, you say? You want more, then?"

"Please."

He continued the pattern. Two slaps and then his fingers inside me.

"Please," I begged again, so close to coming. I watched Cortez lean back on his haunches as though he was studying my wetness. He leaned forward.

"Come in my mouth, Kensington." I shattered immediately only to come again when he thrust his cock inside me. Watching his face, I knew the minute his orgasm hit, as powerful as mine had been.

He held me in his arms for a long while afterwards, and I wished I knew what he was thinking.

When my eyes opened again, Cortez was staring at me.

"How long was I asleep?"

"Not long."

His gaze was so intense, it was unnerving. "Cortez?"

"What we did earlier, it excited you?"

My cheeks flushed. "Very much. Wasn't it obvious?"

He brought his lips to mine and kissed me hard.

"Kensington."

I smiled at the way he often said my name. Like a statement. "Yes?"

He brought both hands to my breasts and toyed with my nipples. He pinched and then licked them, sucked and then twisted them. No matter what he did, it sent an electrical current straight through to my pussy.

"You are so responsive to me. I like that."

"I like it too," I said, arching my back when he sucked one hard nipple into his mouth. It hurt, and at the same time, it felt like no pleasure I'd known before.

"There is so much I want to do to your body."

The way he said it, a shiver went through me.

"You are not afraid."

"I'm not," I said, even though he hadn't phrased his words as a question.

He grinned. "Perhaps you should be."

I took his hand and put it between my legs. "Do I feel like I'm afraid?" He pushed me to my side and entered me from the back. Seconds later, I was climaxing, and so was he.

I could stay in this room, both of us naked, all day. Several days in a row, in fact, but what must his mother and father be thinking. I rolled my eyes and groaned.

Cortez laughed. "What was that for?"

"Your mother. Do you think she knows what we're doing?"

He shook his head. "No, I do not."

"Thank God."

"Are you feeling shameful, Kensington?"

"Only in that I was just thinking I could stay in bed with you for days on end and never want to leave."

"Would you like to stay on here for a few days or return to Mallorca?"

I smiled, wondering if he could read my mind.

"Ah, I see."

I laughed out loud. "You can read my mind!"

He kissed my neck. "It doesn't work exactly that way. It's more of a feeling I get. Unless there's something specific you want to say to me without saying it out loud."

"Like earlier, when you told me to settle my mind and let you in."

"Exactly."

"Your mother asked if we were staying through Epiphany."

"Is that what you'd like to do?"

"It would be more than a week."

"Through the new year?"

"Less than a week, but close."

"You are not giving me an answer, my darling."

"Your family is very gracious, but to be honest, I really love being at your house on Mallorca."

"There is no place on earth I'd rather be, especially if I'm with you."

In the end, we agreed to stay for a few more days, but not as long as *Fiesta de los Reyes*.

New Year's Eve at the palace was spectacular. There was a huge ball, and I was told there would be fireworks at midnight.

I'd brought nothing appropriate to wear, but Maya, Cortez's brother's wife, had plenty of gowns I could choose from, and as we discovered, we wore the same size. She also offered to let me get ready in her dressing area, saying that the two of us could make a grand entrance into the ball together.

"I've longed for him to find someone who makes him happy," she said as we looked through her formal dresses.

"This…thing between us is very new," I said, pulling one that caught my eye off the rack.

"Cortez will love you in that one," she said when I came out a few minutes later. The gown I chose draped over one shoulder and had a wide satin sash at the waist. The Georgette fabric was a pale lavender on top and transitioned to peach. It was long and flowing, which was perfect since I was more than a couple of inches taller than Maya.

"You should leave your hair down. It's so dramatic with its length."

When I spoke with Teagon earlier about the ball, she reminded me she was working and wouldn't have felt at all comfortable attending as a guest. While I still felt odd about it, she assured me she didn't.

Maya had chosen a dark purple raw-silk gown. With her darker skin, hair, and eyes, she was striking in it.

When we came down the grand staircase of the residence, Cortez and his brother were waiting for us at the bottom.

He grasped my hands when I stood in front of him. "You look magnificent," he murmured, kissing my neck right below my ear. I shuddered. "It's as though the gown was made for you."

"Doesn't she look lovely?" said Maya, taking my hand.

"I'm happy for you, Cortez," I heard his brother say. "I could not imagine a woman more perfect for you."

"You have enchanted my family. It seems everyone is taken with you."

"Cortez…" I slowed so his brother and wife were several paces in front of us. "Do comments like those of your brother bother you?"

He put his hand on my bare shoulder, stroking my skin with his fingers. "He speaks the truth."

I felt my cheeks flush and looked away. Cortez moved his fingertips to my chin and turned my head to face him. "They all speak the truth, Kensington."

I shook my head. "But…"

"As I feared, this is too soon for you."

"It isn't that."

"No?"

"Celestina was your wife."

With his other hand, he brought my palm to his lips and kissed it. "An evening such as this would not have been possible with her."

I felt my eyes fill with tears. "Why not?" I whispered.

"She wasn't comfortable socializing with my family."

"I'm sorry."

"Don't be. That is in the past."

"Come on, you two," I heard Maya shout. "Kensington and I are making an entrance."

Cortez raised a brow and smiled. "Kindred spirit?"

"She's very gracious."

"Reminds me of someone else I know. You were wonderful with the families at the hospital on Christmas night."

"My heart broke for them."

"You soothed them."

"Did I? I wanted to do more. In fact, I absolutely love the idea. I would love to initiate the same kind of thing, perhaps in London." Cortez tried to hide it, but I saw him flinch. "I didn't mean…"

"Come, the ball awaits."

When the clock struck midnight, Cortez and I began the new year in one another's arms with a passionate kiss. Not long after, we thanked the King and Queen and then excused ourselves for a night of more mind-blowing sex.

Two days later, I accidentally walked in on a conversation between Cortez and his mother.

"I fear he knows he can get to her on Mallorca," I heard her say.

"She will have protection."

"He will stop at nothing, Cortez."

He murmured, raised his head, and looked into my eyes.

"Why will he stop at nothing?" I asked.

He brushed his lower lip with his finger and looked away. "I do not know."

A chill went through me. Cortez had just lied to me. He knew exactly why Konstantine seemed to be tracking me, and didn't want me to know.

Rile

"Do not let Konstantine out of your sight," I told Smoke. "There is reason to believe he intends to act."

"Roger that."

"Can you speak freely?"

"If you're asking if I'm alone, affirmative."

"How are things going with Siren?"

Smoke made a growling sound.

"That well?"

"Pain in my fucking ass, Rile," he muttered.

"Blame Decker." I laughed and ended the call. I actually couldn't imagine two operatives better suited to work together, once each one let go of their intransigent independence.

My laughter soon faded; Kensington was unhappy with me, and I could guess why. However, until I had a better read on Konstantine, I could not share what I believed his motives to be.

We were scheduled to leave Madrid the next morning, but before I finalize our plans, I wanted to check in with Decker.

"Have you heard anything on Otto von Habsburg's recovery?"

"Negative. It's like the whole family has suddenly gone mute."

"Which means they're covering something up."

"You never know with those damn inbreds." Decker paused, but I sensed he had something else to say. "You okay, Rile?"

I trusted and respected all three of the men I asked to go into partnership with me, but I had to admit, I had a deeper connection with Decker.

"I may be in over my head."

"Understood," he said in a way that made me think he truly did. "Maybe getting your mind on something completely different would do you good."

I had to agree. "If you hear of a mission—something that wouldn't keep me away too long—let me know."

He laughed. "You'll probably hear before I do."

Before our call ended, he said he'd also let me know if he heard anything else out of Budapest, and I agreed to do the same. The other thing I'd agreed with was that, as much as I would've preferred to go home, Kensington would be far safer here at the royal compound than anywhere else.

"Have you seen Kensington?" I asked my mother once my call with Decker ended.

"She and Angel are out walking the grounds. I believe Casper is shadowing them. You're having a hard time keeping everything in the right place."

"That's one way to put it."

"Cortez, the thing about Kensington is, she's…"

"Yes? Go on."

"You've met your match, my dear." My mother stood and walked over to the window. "Please come here, Cortez."

I stood, and she pointed out to where Kensington sat talking to Angel.

"She's bright, extraordinarily beautiful, and unlike her mother, doesn't care about money."

Likely why her grandparents left it all to her.

"She has a good heart, my dear son. Like none you've known." She turned to me, I suppose to see if I'd react or perhaps even argue her point, but I didn't, because I agreed. Celestina was the love of my life. I could've lived happily with her until I took my last breath, but there was no telling what trajectory my life would've taken.

"But I never would've challenged you the way she does."

The two of you are different.

"I couldn't read you when I was alive, Cort. She can."

My mother's face wore an indulgent smile.

"I feel conspired against."

She patted my hand. "If only everyone had your problems, Cortez. How very awful for you that the conspiracy is to make you see how much love you have in your life."

"Love, Mother?"

"If you think she doesn't love you, then you are not as smart as I've always believed you to be."

"Excuse me." My mobile rang with a call from Grinder, and I left the room to take it.

"There's a situation in Italy I need your help with," he began. By the time the call ended, I knew I had no choice but to go myself. Why had I tempted fate in my conversation with Decker when I all but wished for a mission to get me out of here?

If time were not of the essence, it might have been possible to call in additional support in terms of independent operatives to assist Grinder. The only ones currently in Europe were already working ops—for me.

With Smoke and Siren on Konstantine's detail and Angel and Casper along with the King's entire security team on Kensington's, it made the most sense that I be the one to go.

It wasn't a decision easily made. However, whether it was when I was with MI6, or now, on my own, there were times when any agent had to make difficult choices. This was one of those times.

Before returning to continue my conversation with my mother, I rang Angel.

"There's a situation I need to discuss with you and Casper. Where is Kensington?"

"She's resting."

"And Casper?"

"Outside her door."

"Very well, I'll meet with you now, and then you can brief Casper."

"Sounds urgent."

"I've no idea how long I'll be gone," I said when she met me in the courtyard and I briefed her on the situation in Italy. "I'll be back as quickly as I can be. Before I leave, I'll instruct Smoke to brief you regarding the situation with Konstantine as often as necessary."

"If I may," she said.

"By all means."

"We have things covered here, Rile. As far as Kensington is concerned, there is no place more secure, other than perhaps Buckingham Palace."

I agreed. However, that didn't make my decision to leave her any easier, particularly since we were at odds.

"You said Kensington is resting."

"Yes. She asked not to be disturbed."

I brushed my lower lip with my fingertip. "Very well. Please let her know of my departure and that I hope to return within a few days at the most."

"I'll be leaving for Italy within the hour," I said when I rejoined my mother in the sitting room. "One of my partners has requested my help on an investigation."

"You forget to whom you're speaking, Cortez."

"Kensington is in good hands here, Duchess."

"I agree. How long will you be gone?"

I stepped forward and kissed her cheek. "I don't yet know, but I'll keep you informed." I went to the stairs to pack a bag, and she followed.

"Cortez, Kensington will be safe here."

I had to trust that she would be.

17

Kensington

"You put me in a terrible position," Teagon said after she told me Cortez left.

"He lied to me. He knows something about Konstantine, and he refused to tell me what it was."

"I am certain he has a good reason, namely, your protection, Kenz."

"He could've said that very thing, but he chose not to."

"It's the way it works. As Casper and I have explained to you, there are times when it is better if the person we are protecting is unaware of what might be happening behind the scenes."

"I disagree with that methodology."

Teagon laughed. "Too bloody bad, Kenz. It's the way it has to be."

"Why is he going to Italy?"

"There's an investigation, and that's as much as I know."

"Now, you're lying."

"I am not. However, if you hadn't behaved so child-ishly, you could've asked him yourself."

I stuck my tongue out, showing her exactly how childish I could be. "I'm going for a walk."

"I'll go with you."

I wanted more than anything to be on my own, which for now, appeared impossible.

"Oh, good. I was about to come looking for you," said Cortez's mother when Teagon and I came down the stairs. "I was hoping you and I could have a chat, Kensington."

Why did I feel as though I was about to be scolded?

Teagon nodded and stood in the doorway when the duchess put her arm through mine and ushered me into the sitting room.

"Don't worry, you've done nothing wrong," she said as she motioned for me to take a seat. "Would you like some tea?"

"Please."

She pressed a button on her mobile and then sat beside me and took my hands in hers.

"I owe you an apology."

I started to shake my head and say she didn't, but she shushed me.

"Cortez and I share a…unique bond. I sense that perhaps you may share it as well."

"I'm not sure."

"Yes, well, in the beginning, it can be difficult to ascertain what is highly attuned intuition and what you could not possibly know." She took a deep breath. "Back to Cortez and I. We sometimes speak in short-hand, if that makes any sense."

"It does."

"It drives my husband and other son a bit bonkers, but there is little that Cort and I can do about it. What you walked in on was that very thing."

"He lied to me."

"Yes, he did. That is the reason for my apology."

"You didn't lie; he did."

She shrugged. "It's all a matter of how you look at it. I came to Cortez with a concern that, to anyone else, might have seemed unfounded. I had no proof of what von Habsburg was thinking or planning. What I had was a feeling."

"He could've said."

"Perhaps with you, he could've. But with most, he could not. It's what he's accustomed to. He protects me, if you will."

"And you do the same for him."

She squeezed my hand. "That's right. Not everyone is accepting of our methodologies."

I laughed and looked over my shoulder; Teagon was laughing too. "I just said something quite similar."

"Forgive him, Kensington."

I felt ashamed of myself for both my reaction and my treatment of him.

"And try to forgive yourself too."

"This will take some getting used to—having someone who can so easily read my thoughts."

She raised a brow. "I believe you know how to stop it from happening. Don't you?"

"Wow. Seriously?"

"It was very effective, my dear."

Two days later, as I lay awake until the early morning hours, worried about Cortez, wondering if he was safe, I continued to berate myself for my foolish and, yes, childish behavior.

"I hope you're keeping him safe," I said out loud in the empty room. Only silence echoed back to me.

I got out of bed, put on my joggers, and went out in the hallway, intending to get some exercise. Casper was outside my door.

"Good Lord, have you been there all night?"

She nodded.

"Is that necessary?"

"When the boss is away? Absolutely."

"I'm off on a run."

She motioned for me to go ahead, and stayed a maximum of ten paces behind me. I suppose it might've been nice for me to strike up a conversation with her, but I wasn't in the mood. The only person I wanted to talk to was Cortez. I had only myself to blame for not being able to.

The palace grounds, much like those of my great-aunt, the Queen's, offered fantastic trails to run. Like there, I knew security was always close by, and not just Casper. No harm would come to me while on this property, nor would I cause that of another. The security team was protecting the royal family from me as much as me from anyone else.

I was nearing the edge of the compound when I heard people shouting behind me. I stopped to look, but Casper stood in my way.

"Keep going," she barked.

"But—"

"Kensington, keep moving!" This time, she shouted.

I picked up my pace as did she. We were almost back to Cortez's parents' residence when Teagon met us.

"Get her inside," Casper told her before taking off in the direction from which we came.

"What's going on?" I asked once we were inside.

My lifelong best friend's eyes scrunched. "I cannot tell you now. You must respect that."

I felt bloody awful that she had to point that out to me. I knew better; I'd been in close proximity to royalty my entire life. "My apologies."

"Accepted."

I didn't see Casper at all for the rest of the day. In fact, I saw almost no one other than Teagon and a few of the servants. I was about to drift off while reading when I heard someone come in the front door.

"Where is she?" I heard Cortez shout.

"In here," Teagon said in a loud voice, and I stood.

Cortez rushed over and wrapped me in his arms. "Thank God, you're safe," he said, kissing me. He turned and looked at Teagon. "We're returning to Mallorca tonight. Please make arrangements."

"Cortez?" I heard his mother's voice. "Do you think that's wise?"

"Yes." He put his arm around my waist. "Come, we'll collect our things and leave."

"I'd like to say goodbye and thank the rest of your family."

"There isn't time. You'll see them again."

There was a tremendous amount of tension surrounding us, so much so that it was frightening me. When we entered the room upstairs and Cortez closed the door behind us, I asked, "Will you tell me what happened this afternoon?"

He scrubbed his face with his hand. "I suppose I must."

I sat on the end of the bed, and he sat beside me.

"Konstantine attempted to access the grounds today."

"Attempted to access?"

"He contacted the King's staff, asking for an audience. When it was refused, he tried to force his way on the property."

"I think it's time you tell me what is really going on with Konstantine von Habsburg."

"I shall. As much as I know. But not until we are safely back on Mallorca."

18

Rile

I couldn't fault Smoke and Siren as much as I wished I could, just to give way to anger at myself. I had left Kensington, a woman under my protection, to go to Italy. In fact, I'd been anxious for the mission—any mission.

The two people I'd put on Konstantine's detail were the ones who alerted palace security that he was attempting to meet with the King as well as of his actions once the meeting was refused.

He'd been arrested, but soon, his father would arrange for his release, given the son would have diplomatic immunity.

Kensington demanded I tell her what Konstantine's motives were, and I'd agreed. However, I didn't know. Not for certain, anyway. As far as getting a read on the man, it was nearly impossible, given the depths of madness to which he'd descended.

His desperation to make Kensington his wife confused me. While not rich like any of the reigning monarchs, the von Habsburgs were wealthy, and upon his parents' deaths, Konstantine would inherit a great deal of money. So it didn't make sense that he would be after her wealth. Yes, along with it, she was extraordinarily beautiful, smart, and had ties to the royal family in the UK. Was that enough for a madman? Could what seemed to defy logic for a sane person, not register with a mentally ill man?

Apart from Kensington, I remained convinced that Konstantine was responsible for the attack on his cousin, but was unable to prove it. Smoke's report that Otto had come out of his coma and was ready to talk, was erroneous. As a result of his injuries, Otto had suffered a stroke and, for the time being, couldn't speak. Reports indicated he would, eventually, but that meant we had no choice but to wait until he regained the ability.

Rather than keeping them on Konstantine's detail, I asked both Smoke and Siren to join us on Mallorca. I'd also enlisted the services of two other operatives, Ink and Crash. I felt far more comfortable having people I trusted on my team at home. I accepted the MI6 assistance Z offered to cover von Habsburg.

Prior to our departure, my mother assembled the members of our immediate family so Kensington could say goodbye and thank her and my father as well as my brother and Maya. My nephews put their arms around her neck and begged her to come visit again. I didn't recall seeing her with them other than at family meals; however, she'd made a lasting impression. Not just with them, but my other family members appeared similarly emotional upon my insistence that we must leave.

Angel transported us back to Mallorca via helicopter. Only her, Casper, Kensington, and I traveled together. I'd sent Smoke and Siren ahead of us shortly after Konstantine's arrest, so when we arrived at the airfield, they'd already be there. Ink and Crash were on their way from the States.

Kensington was as subdued as I'd expected her to be. I had no intention of pressing her to be anything but. She had a lot of questions, not all that I'd have answers to, and that would leave her unsettled.

Her comfort was my main reason for returning to Mallorca. A security team could be put in place anywhere, including my uncle's compound. However, I knew she'd be able to relax more being in my home than anywhere else.

We drove straight to the house upon our arrival at the airfield. Once there, Kensington informed me she was going for a swim. I gave her a few minutes and then joined her in the indoor pool. The pace at which she was swimming told me more about her level of stress than I could intuit. When she stopped at the end where I stood, she was out of breath. She was also angry.

I sat down on the pool's edge and dangled my feet in the water; she removed her goggles.

"Tell me who you're most angry with."

"Myself," she responded without hesitation. "If I hadn't gone to Budapest in the first place, this would not have happened."

"I'm not certain that is the case."

"It was as though the minute I agreed, he decided we'd marry. He even said it."

"When?"

"While he was trying to rape me."

"Tell me his exact words. Or as best as you can remember."

"He had me pinned against the wall, and I was trying to get away from him. That's when he said, '*By tomorrow evening, you'll be my wife and mine to do with as I please.*'"

"Remind me, you'd been in Budapest less than a week?"

"That's right."

"How long was it between the time you agreed and your departure?"

"A couple of hours."

"Which meant he'd planned to marry you prior to you agreeing to go with him."

"I don't understand."

"Hungarian law requires a ten-day waiting period between license issuance and marriage."

"Why would he want to marry me? He doesn't even know me. The only thing that makes sense is that it would be for my money."

"That is certainly a possibility."

"Even if we wed, he'd never get his hands on it. It's managed by a trust, and any marriage I enter into would require an ironclad prenup."

"Have you spoken with your mother since your abrupt departure?"

She smiled when I did. "Ironclad prenup and Kiki go hand in hand. And in answer to your question, no, I haven't, and she's fit to be tied. The last I heard from her, she was preparing to disown me." Her eyes opened wide. "You want me to contact her, don't you?"

"She seemed anxious for an alliance between him and you. I've wondered about her motivation."

"Her only motivation is that she's anxious for me to marry. I doubt she cares to whom, just that I get on with it."

"Why is that?"

Kensington shrugged. "I've never understood it apart from the fact that if I married, I'd be someone else's problem. That in itself makes no sense, given I've never relied on her for much of anything. She certainly doesn't support me."

I thought back to our conversation on Christmas Eve when I told her she was the daughter of two people who cared about her very much—her grandparents. They'd obviously shown her immeasurable love in that she didn't seem particularly sad when she spoke of her parents' lack of involvement in her life.

I took a deep breath, troubled that I couldn't figure out what lay behind Konstantine's desperation. Later, I'd give Decker a call and ask him to do some digging. For now, though, I owed Kensington an apology.

I slid into the water and put my arms around her waist. "I'm sorry I didn't answer you when you over-heard my conversation with my mother."

"She already apologized."

"Did she?"

Kensington nodded. "She said you were protecting her."

"Interesting," I murmured. I suppose, to a certain extent, doing so was innate. "I don't have to with you, do I?"

"I can't say that I understand completely, but I've seen enough evidence of it to know that you and your mother do seem to have a sixth sense about certain things."

"As do you."

"I don't know that I'd go that far."

"Either way, I'm sorry."

"You aren't used to answering questions." Kensington kissed my neck under my ear.

"That is true."

"Can we stop talking about unpleasantries now?"

"Of course." I put my hands under her bottom and lifted so her legs wrapped around my waist. "I don't like it when we're at odds with one another."

"I don't either. I missed you so much."

Her words were like a stab to my heart. "I'm sorry for the way I left. I'm sorry that I left you at all."

"Why did you?"

"Because I'm a bloody idiot." I kissed her, hard, holding the back of her head with one hand while the other held her arse.

It had been four days since I was inside of her, and I needed her like a man starving. "Come," I said, lifting her onto the pool deck and then hoisting myself out of the water. My rock-hard cock strained for release inside my swimsuit. Kensington cupped it with her hand.

We dripped water on the floor of the lift as I pushed her up against the back panel and ground myself against her.

When it stopped on the top floor, I carried her into the bedroom. There were eyes everywhere; I knew because I put them there, but Kensington's naked body was for mine alone. I closed the blinds throughout the suite.

Our bodies were chilled from the pool's water. I turned on the shower and led her inside once it was warm. "Put your hands on the wall."

She complied, and I removed her swimsuit. I turned her around in the warm water and pressed her back against the tile.

After removing my own suit, I lifted her again and entered her with one thrust. Kensington cried out as I pounded into her, and her wetness engulfed my cock.

I kept her in bed the rest of the afternoon, pleasuring her body again and again. Every so often, I'd run warm water in the jetted tub and let it soothe us.

"I couldn't imagine a place more perfect," she said as we watched the storm clouds roll in over the sea. "It looks so ominous, almost dangerous, and yet here we are, safe and warm."

From where I sat, I could see the cemetery where Celestina rested, but I couldn't feel her presence. I hadn't for days.

Kensington was swirling the water with her hands. Her, I could feel. Her soft skin, her warm heart, and her troubled mind.

"Is there something you want to ask me?" When she shook her head, I nipped her ear. "Do not lie to me, my darling."

She turned her head enough that she could look at me. "Marta said there was a baby."

I closed my eyes, knowing Kensington could feel my pain. "Yes," I whispered.

"I'm sorry, Cortez."

I shook my head, and a tear fell down my cheek. For every moment I mourned Celestina, I mourned our unborn child twice as much. I knew it was a boy, not because a doctor confirmed it, just because I knew.

He would be the same age as my brother's oldest son. I'd never told anyone about the baby. I sensed my mother knew, but she'd never said anything either.

The only person who had known Celestina was pregnant at the time of her death was Marta, and I wasn't upset with her for telling Kensington. I can't say whether I ever would have or not. That she did know, soothed me, though.

"Can I ask you something?"

I looked into the warmth of her amber eyes. "Anything."

"Do you want to have children someday?"

If anyone other than Kensington had asked, I would've said I didn't see myself becoming a father. Or maybe it wasn't "other than her," maybe it was before her.

"I would like that very much. What about you?"

"If you had asked me that a few months ago, I would've said I didn't see myself becoming a mother."

I kissed her cheek, unable to hold in my laughter.

"What? Is that funny?"

"Not at all, it's just that I thought those same words, almost exactly. How do you feel now, my darling?"

"I worry that I wouldn't be good at it. You know, because of Kiki."

"But you aren't Kiki's daughter. You're Bea's."

"I know we've talked about that, but do you really think I was influenced more by my grandmother than my mother?"

"In every way."

"What makes you so certain?"

"If I were to meet you and Kiki at the same time, same place, I wouldn't guess you are related at all. You're nothing alike. You don't look alike, and you certainly don't act like her."

"She always seemed like an annoying older sister. One I didn't have to see very often."

"What about your father?"

She was swirling the water with her hands again. "He has a good heart, albeit a selfish one."

"It is good you recognize it for what it is."

"Kiki was pregnant when they got married. They were engaged for a year, so it wasn't as though I was the only reason they got married. But sometimes I wonder if she hadn't been pregnant, if he would've gone through with it. From what Gran Bea told me, it wasn't long after, that his career took off."

"How many would you want?"

"Children?"

"Yes."

She shrugged and laughed. "I don't know."

"Come on. You thought of a number. Say it out loud."

"Four."

"Why four?"

"Four bedrooms."

"Ah. I see. We could have more if they shared rooms."

"Good point."

I expected Kensington to balk, but she didn't. She didn't even flinch. Was it possible that this could be my life? Could happiness truly be close enough for me to touch?

Kensington turned her body and faced me. She put her hands on my face and looked into my eyes. "Yes, it truly can be."

19

Kensington

Teagon sat down next to me with her plate of breakfast foods. "The two of you are so happy, it's bloody annoying."

"Agreed," muttered Casper from the other end of the table.

"I won't apologize for it."

Teagon covered my hand with hers. "I was joking."

"I wasn't," said Casper.

"Ignore her," my best friend whispered under her breath. Casper got up and left, which didn't bother me in the least.

"Is it really necessary for her to be here?"

"That isn't my decision, Kenz."

"Maybe I'll talk to Cortez about it."

"If he refuses, understand that it's only—"

"For my protection. I understand." I looked over my shoulder to make sure no one else was in the room with us. "Have you met the others?"

With wide eyes, she nodded slowly.

"And?"

"I'm considering his offer to leave MI6 and come work for him."

"Seriously? Why? I mean, I know why, but…you know what I mean."

She put one hand on her hip. "Yes, Kenz, what you mean is I'm a catch."

"I'd say." I threw a handful of blueberries into my mouth. "What about it, then? Would you?"

"Maybe. It shouldn't matter, but the pay he offered is quite good."

"Why shouldn't it matter? If it's your job, you should be paid your worth." I shook my head. "Says the person who's never held a job in her life. Ignore me."

"No, you're right. It isn't that MI6 doesn't pay well; it does. It's just that going private appears to pay better."

"What about meeting the others made you say you're considering a change?"

"Oh, right." She looked over her shoulder like I had. "Kenzie, have you seen them?"

"Them?"

"The other two agents Rile put on your detail."

"I thought there were four."

"There are, but two seem to be a couple, sort of. They fight like one. Anyway, it's the other two men I'm speaking of."

"I've only seen them from a distance."

"You know I have no interest whatsoever in Rile, right?"

I scrunched my eyes. "Yes, but why would you preface it with such a statement?"

"Because he's bloody hot, that's why."

"True."

"These other two are hotter. Way hotter."

I smiled and winked. "I find that impossible to believe."

"For you, maybe, since these gents are under thirty."

I slugged her arm. "So…hot, eh?"

"One more than the other, but *gawd*."

"Maybe you'll get your next *best kiss ever* soon."

She shook her head. "Not a chance. We're working, but when this is over, who knows?"

My face fell, and I couldn't hide it.

Teagon put her hand on my arm. "What?"

"I said 'soon.'"

"Yeah?"

"And you said not a chance."

"Oh, I see. You took that to mean that this won't be over soon."

"Doesn't it?"

"I guess there's no way of knowing. At least not yet."

"Can't someone just lock Konstantine up? Or can't I get a restraining order or something?"

"Not a lot of good that would do, and no, he's got diplomatic immunity."

"Why? He's not a diplomat."

"Respect for a previous monarch, I guess."

"So he can behave like a lunatic and just gets away with it? Surely, King Ferdinand could've done something."

"You know how it is."

"What does that mean?"

"Diplomacy. Politics. Looking the other way when it comes to royals."

I suppose I did. Although I was glad to see some comeuppance as of late. Particularly with my one "cousin" who fraternized with the sex slave trafficker. He might not be in jail, but he had certainly become *persona non grata*.

Teagon swiped a handful of blueberries from my bowl. "What about after, Kenz? What happens between you and Rile?"

"I don't know," I said barely above a whisper. Should I tell her we talked about kids?

"*Buenos días*," said Marta, coming off the lift.

"Good morning, Marta," I said, standing to hug her. "Welcome back. Did you have a nice holiday?"

She shrugged and got a sad look. "As nice as it can be now, I suppose."

I felt like someone had punched me in the stomach with all their might, and grabbed the kitchen counter to steady myself.

"I'm sorry, Marta. I didn't realize."

She patted my cheek with her palm. "You have nothing to be sorry for, sweetheart. It does my heart good to see Cortez happy again."

"See you later, Marta!" called out Teagon, motioning me toward the lift. "What was that about?" she asked once the door closed behind us.

"Celestina was Marta's daughter."

"How…" She shook her head. "You scare me sometimes."

I felt ill and wrapped my arms around my stomach. When we got to the fourth floor, I followed her into the bedroom and flopped on the bed.

"Are you okay?"

I buried my head in the pillow. "I don't think so."

A few minutes passed before Teagon or I spoke again. "Kenz?"

I turned my head to look at her.

"What about Konstantine? I mean, could you…did you know…"

"What was he thinking?" I thought about the way I felt that night when we were at the bar and how I'd known intuitively not to cross him. Was it because I was reading something someone else might not see, or was it just what I'd witnessed with others?

"Could you?" she asked again.

"I'm not certain."

"What about me? Do you know what I'm thinking?"

"It's too disturbing. I block you."

Her eyes opened wider.

"I'm kidding. *Gawd,* Teag. It's not an all-the-time thing. And it isn't necessarily knowing what someone is thinking. It's a combination of reaction and body language and intuition."

"There's no way you could've known that Rile's deceased wife was Marta's daughter."

"No? Not even when a look of sadness came over her face and she said, 'as nice as it can be now'? Honestly, I think that was mainly intuition."

"It's interesting to think about, yes? Do you have a sixth sense, or are you just really good at reading people? Whichever it is, Kenz, it's unnerving."

I stood and shook my arms and legs. "I need some exercise, and you do too if you want to impress these hotter-than-Cortez guys you were talking about."

"Thanks a lot, *mate*."

"Come on, let's go do something. I'm going crazy just sitting around."

We went for a swim, and then I ran on the treadmill while Teagon lifted weights.

"That didn't help," I grumbled.

"How far did you run?"

I looked over at the display on the treadmill. "Five miles."

"If that didn't help, I don't know what will."

I wiggled my eyebrows. "I do."

"Can't help you there, girlfriend."

"I can," said Cortez, coming around the corner and scaring the *bejesus* out of me. He walked over and put his arm around me.

"I'm all sweaty."

"The way I like you best," he whispered, licking my neck.

"That will be my cue to leave. Thanks for the workout, Kenz." She looked at Cortez and, when he nodded, walked out of the workout room.

"I'm sorry I've been too busy to spend time with you today."

"Don't be. It isn't up to you to entertain me."

"I like entertaining you very much." He wiggled his eyebrows like I had.

I smiled and sat down on one of the lifting benches.

"Something is on your mind."

I wiped my sweaty face with a towel. "Do you know that, or are you guessing, or do you already know what I'm thinking?"

He sat next to me. "I can tell there's something on your mind because you seem tense. I cannot read your mind, Kensington. When I know what you're thinking, it's because you want me to. Even then, it's a feeling."

"Sometimes, I think I hear your words in my head."

"Yes, it can be that way."

"Doesn't it make you crazy?"

"It isn't any different than when you and I are talking. I can choose to still my mind and listen to what you're saying because I very much want to know. There are other times there's a great deal on my mind, and I'm not paying attention the way I should. It's the same for everyone, I think."

"It's just that you hear more than only what people say."

"Not always. But back to my question, Kensington, is there something on your mind you'd like to discuss with me?"

I looked down at my feet, thinking that I was going to need a new pair of running shoes soon. "I feel like I'm in limbo."

"I understand. When can you get back to a life that feels more normal?"

"I'm not sure I know what that even means. Not since Gran Bea died. It's just that I've never been someone who needed round-the-clock security. My grandmother did, and it was second nature to her."

He was quiet, thoughtful, and I appreciated that he wouldn't give me an off-the-cuff answer.

"I wish I could read your mind right now."

Cortez smiled. "I am conflicted."

Not what I expected. "Why?"

"I very much like having you here."

I felt my cheeks flush. "I like being here."

"But you wish you could have more freedom."

"Doesn't everyone desire to go for a walk alone?" I picked my foot up from the floor and rotated my ankle. "Or buy new running shoes when they need them?"

"We will take care of as many of your desires as we are able to. Some will be easier than others."

The one question I wanted to ask, I couldn't bring myself to. I was too afraid of his answer.

Cortez took my hand and pulled me to my feet. He put his arms around me and stared into my eyes. "I want you to be here with me because it's where you want to be, not because you have to be."

"That's what I want as well."

"Know that I am doing everything in my power to make that happen."

20

Rile

By the end of January, I knew Kensington was restless. No matter how hard she tried to hide it from everyone else, she couldn't possibly hide it from me.

I had taken her to the same bistro for her birthday where I took her on Christmas Eve. When I told her to make a wish and blow out the candles, she gave me an idea I'd been painstakingly working to make happen.

As far as the von Habsburgs, I was frustrated by the lack of information regarding Otto's recovery since I was certain that questioning him about his attack would lead to a revelation about why his cousin seemed obsessed with Kensington.

The diplomatic immunity Konstantine enjoyed meant law enforcement was unable to hold him after an arrest. Within hours, he was a free man.

As was so often the case, it then fell upon those same authorities to keep the victim—in this case, Kensington—a virtual prisoner in order to keep them safe.

I hoped the surprise I had planned for her would raise her spirits. It took a tremendous amount of planning, including making arrangements with my father to use his plane, given the distance I intended to travel.

Prior to that, it took a lot of convincing—and more than a lot of money—to make sure we had the entire island to ourselves.

With everything now in place, we were slated to leave on the first of February. All that was left to do was inform Kensington.

I found her sitting by the infinity pool, reading a book. When she set it in her lap and looked up at me, I leaned down and kissed her.

"There's something on your mind," she said, winking.

I sat down beside her when she scooted over on the chaise. "I have a surprise for you."

Her eyes lit up.

"We're taking a trip."

"Are you going to tell me where?"

"I'd rather keep that a surprise as well. However, I want to reassure you that we are not going to America."

She laughed. "As long as you're not taking me back to Kiki's, I can wait. Should I pack?"

"Yes. Plan for balmy weather."

"I like it already."

When I leaned forward and kissed her again, she put her arms around my neck. "Thank you, Cortez."

"You're welcome, my darling."

The next morning, as we drove in a caravan to the airfield, a feeling of dread settled over me, and I rubbed my chest. Kensington must've noticed since she rested her hand on mine and squeezed my fingers.

Once at the airfield, I reviewed our flight plan along with the plan for security once we landed at our destination.

I'd been intentional in choosing the seven-hundred-and-forty-acre island because it was private with very little accessibility. That didn't mean it was one-hundred percent secure; nothing ever could be. However, with the team I had assembled, I believed we would be able to keep Kensington safe. There would be staff working where we'd be staying, but each person employed had been thoroughly vetted by Decker.

I rolled my shoulders as I climbed the steps to the plane where Kensington had already gotten settled. As prearranged, when I walked into the main cabin, there was a buffet of food set out along with bottles of champagne.

I looked around for Kensington, who moments later, walked out of one of two staterooms and smiled. I opened my arms and met her halfway. She put her arms around my neck and kissed me. "This is bloody brilliant, Cortez. Thank you."

I cupped her cheek with my palm. "It's nice to see your smile."

We ate while the crew prepared for our departure. Once they and the team were in place and the buffet stored away, she and I went to the aft cabin for take-off.

"Is it a long flight?"

"Yes. Would you like to know how long?"

Kensington shook her head. "Nope."

I held her hand, marveling at the trust she placed in me. We'd had long talks about the length of time I believed it would be necessary for her to stay under the protection of a full team. After her questions were answered, she accepted them without argument.

Once we heard the chimes indicating we could move about the aircraft, she stood and held her hand out to me. I followed her into the stateroom, locked the door behind me, and watched as she pulled her simple shift over her head and tossed it on the chair. Underneath, she wore a royal-blue bra and panty set.

"Please, let me," I said when she reached up to undo the clasp between her two magnificent breasts. Kensington smiled and dropped her hands. "Lie on the bed, my darling. Spread your legs for me." She shuddered, and chill bumps covered her arms and legs. Not to worry, though, within a few short minutes, she'd be burning with the fiery passion that always ignites between us.

I slowly removed my clothes, placing them on the chair where she'd tossed her dress. Once naked, I crawled beside her and wrapped my hand around the back of her neck, holding her tightly to me as our tongues intertwined. She grasped my steel-hard cock, and I hissed with pleasure before grabbing her wrist and moving her hand away.

"Cortez," she moaned, the lower half of her body writhing.

"Put your hands above your head, Kensington, and leave them there. Do not move them unless I tell you to."

I smiled when she did as I asked with a raised brow. "I want to touch you, Cortez."

"And you shall, when I grant you permission to."

When she squeezed her thighs together, I spread them farther apart, grabbed hold of the side of her panties, and ripped them from her body. The mewl she released told me exactly how much that excited her.

"Look at me, Kensington," I said when her eyes drifted closed. "Watch what I do to you." When I unfastened the clasp, the cups of her bra fell to each side, exposing her luscious tits. Her chest heaved, and her nipples stood erect, begging for my touch.

"Are you wet for me?" I asked, slowly trailing my fingers down the center of her body and then back up. She mewled again, this time in frustration.

"Show me."

"What?"

"I said, show me." I moved one of her hands from above her head and placed it on her pussy. I reached for her other hand and moved it to her breast. "Pinch your nipple and then show me how wet it makes you."

I watched as her fingers spread open her folds and she dragged them through her wetness. I grabbed her wrist and brought her fingers to my mouth, groaning as I sucked her essence from them. "More."

I caught a hint of a smile as she followed my command, wetting her fingers and then bringing her hand back to my mouth.

"Keep pinching your nipple, sweetheart." I sucked her fingers clean a second time and then captured her hard nipple between my teeth. Kensington's back arched, and she cried out with the bite of pain.

"Do you like that?" I asked.

"Do it again," she whispered.

I moved to her other breast and sunk my teeth into its fleshy side. "Put your fingers in your pussy," I demanded before sucking hard on her nipple and while I rubbed circles on her clit with my thumb.

"Harder," I whispered in her ear. I captured her sounds of pleasure when my mouth covered hers and she came.

I pinched her clit when she tried to move my hand away. "Too sensitive, my darling?"

Kensington's hand grasped my wrist as I reached down and thrust two fingers inside her.

"God, Cortez, please."

"Please what, my beauty?"

Her eyes met mine. "Fuck me."

"Say it again."

"Fuck me. Hard. I'm begging you."

I rolled her over, pulled her up at the waist, and thrust inside her drenched heat. She was so tight around me, the perfect size to squeeze my girth as I moved in and out with a slowness that was as painful for me as I knew it was for her.

"Harder," she begged, pushing herself against me.

"Not yet." I kept the same slow, maddening pace until I felt her relax into the rhythm. As soon as she did, I withdrew despite her cry of protest, put my arm around her waist, and rolled her to her back. I raised her legs, holding them together at her ankles and entered her with a single, brutal thrust. "Breathe with me, Kensington."

She looked into my eyes and concentrated on matching her breathing to mine. I pushed deeper into her and held myself there, focusing on her breath, the look in her eyes. She squeezed me with her pussy, and I nipped her ankle, making her giggle and do it again.

I thrust harder then, ramming into her and watching her expression change from playful to lost in a cloud of bliss. Only then did I allow myself to careen over the edge and empty my release deep inside of her.

In a dizzy haze, I dropped beside her, pulling her into my arms. "You are so fucking perfect," I murmured. "You're everything."

I was astounded when I heard the pilot say we were beginning our descent. Kensington and I had pleasured one another's bodies the entire nine-hour trip. Even now, I could barely stand not being back inside of her. I was insatiable. Evidently, she was too, given she reached out and wrapped her hand around my softening cock.

"We have time," she said, pleading with her eyes and taking me into her mouth.

"As if I can resist you."

We were shuttled from the plane to a boat launch where we were quickly transported to the private island of Fregate, the easternmost in the Seychelles.

On the way, the boat's driver educated us on the lush vegetation and told us the largest treehouse in the world sat in one of the island's Banyan trees. We had seven pristine beaches that we only needed to share with the more than two thousand free-roaming, giant Aldabra turtles.

Thatched-roof cottages dotted the hillsides above the dock where the boat would remain for our entire stay. If it became necessary to leave quickly, there was also a helipad on the opposite side of the island with a helicopter on standby.

Angel and Casper stayed with us while the other four team members assisted the island staff in getting our luggage to the cottages I'd designated.

"May I bring you a cocktail?" a woman asked when Kensington and I stepped off the dock, removed our shoes, and made our way to the pristine blue water of the Indian Ocean.

"Outstanding service," Kensington said after we'd placed our order and stepped into the warm water.

"It will continue the entire time we're here."

"And how long will that be?"

"I'm thinking forever might be nice."

She smiled again, which had been my goal. If only there were a place I could keep her safe from harm forever. I knew better, though. Such a place didn't exist. I'd learned that very painful lesson almost seven years ago.

21

Kensington

I woke up in a state of bliss every day we were on the island. Cortez and I went for long walks on the most breathtaking beaches I'd ever seen. We swam in the ocean, made love in secluded coves, ate and drank enough to keep our bodies fueled, and then some.

While he'd said he'd like to stay here forever, he finally confessed we'd be here only a month. I did my best to stay in the moment, enjoy every day, and not think about the most perfect time of my life coming to an end. That became more difficult as time ticked by.

Cortez felt it too; that was easy to see. We'd made a promise, not just between ourselves, but with the entourage—as I began referring to them—we brought with us, that we would not discuss anything to do with the von Habsburgs.

I didn't see them often, but when I did, it was interesting to watch the dynamics between this group of alphas, men and women. Each had a contagious confidence. They were endlessly competitive about everything. When there was a group together, at least one would invent some kind of contest. They ranged from tests of physical strength to self-discipline to who could eat the most or make Cortez and I laugh the hardest. In the midst of it all, they were vigilant about making sure no one who wasn't supposed to be here came onto the island. I was sure they also kept a constant watch on the staff, although they were never intrusive about it.

Smoke and Siren, who appeared to work as a team, walked a very fine line between love and hate. However, both did their absolute best not to let on anything but hate to one another.

Watching the interaction between Teagon and Casper and two of the men who came with us, Ink and Crash, was most fascinating of all. Both treated Casper like a beloved sister, and competed for Teagon's attention.

Ink was the biggest and most fit man I'd ever seen. I could see him competing in Mr. Universe contests—not that I knew whether those still existed. Or just bodybuilding competitions. His muscles literally bulged as if they were straining to tear through the skin that covered them.

Crash was the funniest of the group and was teased endlessly for his code name, which I learned was appropriately given. The man was, in a word, clumsy. I didn't doubt for a minute that he was competent in any kind of dangerous situation, but in day-to-day, normal life, he regularly dropped, ran into, or broke things.

What made the name even worse was that, in addition to being an agent, he was an airline pilot.

He had a long scar running the length of his calf that was the result of a motorcycle accident he'd had in his early twenties. There was a profound sadness surrounding him when Teagon asked what had happened. Later, when Cortez and I were alone, I asked too.

"He was riding with a friend on a mountain road. They came to a blind curve, and a semi-truck coming from the other way hit both motorcycles, sending Crash into the mountainside and his friend off the cliff."

I covered my mouth with my hand. "That's horrifying."

Cortez nodded.

"I don't think you should refer to him as Crash."

He cupped my cheek with his palm. "It's said that acknowledging the loss can help ease the pain of it perhaps better than attempting to block the memory."

"Is that why you visit Celestina's grave so often?"

"In part. As odd as it may seem, it also eased my loneliness."

"Are you anxious to get back?"

He pulled me into him and ran his fingers through my hair. "No more anxious than you are."

"You have a life to return to."

"And you feel as though yours is in limbo."

"More so, yes. It isn't a new thing for me."

He lay back on the bed and held me in his arms. "Tell me, Kensington."

How did I tell him I felt as though my life had no meaning? I had no goals, no purpose. Before Gran Bea passed away, I spent the majority of my time with her. I wasn't her caregiver; she had a staff for that, but I was her companion. I learned more about life—about everything—from her than I ever would have at university.

There were times I wished I'd continued my education, but more because I felt it was expected of me rather than it being something I wanted to do.

Both of my parents graduated from college. My mother from Barnhard, my father from Oxford. Neither did anything with their degrees. My father had a law degree and was a professional photographer. My mother's degree was in literature, and she was a professional socialite.

My grandfather spent his life working in the publishing industry for a house that had been in our family for over three hundred years. He'd worked his way up from a copy boy to chairman of the board, which he sat on until the day he died, at which time the seat was given to me.

After his retirement from daily work, he and my grandmother had labored tirelessly for a variety of social causes.

I realized Cortez was studying me, waiting for an answer to his question.

"I haven't yet found my way." It was something Gran Bea used to say when I would fret about what meaning I had in life. "You will find your way, my dear," she'd say. "And when you do, you'll know instantly that everything went exactly the way it was supposed to go."

Cortez didn't speak, so I continued. "I look at the people with us here on the island, and I find myself envying their level of commitment. Yours too."

"When you find your way, as you said, you will have an equal commitment to it."

"What if I never find it?"

"How hard have you looked?"

"I'm not good at anything, Cortez."

"I beg to differ."

I looked into his eyes to see if he was teasing. "What do you see that I'm good at?"

"You read voraciously, and it is evident in the way you do it that you are learning, soaking it all in. You are very adept in higher societal situations."

"It's a pity I wasn't born in the seventeen hundreds when those talents might have served me."

He brushed my cheek with his finger. "I wasn't finished."

"Thank God."

He laughed and squeezed my shoulder. "You gave immense comfort to the families at the children's hospital on Christmas night. Immense. It isn't just in 'polite company' that you excel; you were marvelous with them."

"And what would I do with such immense talent?"

"Follow your great-aunt's lead as well as that of your grandparents. Find something that speaks to your heart and use your compassion to make a difference."

"I continue Gran Bea's and Huck's charitable work."

"Do you?"

I shook my head. "Not work, no."

"You continue with their level of financial support."

"Yes."

"Why not spend time with each of the organizations and see which you feel compelled to do more for? If it isn't any of those, there are innumerable charities that could use support, either in time, talent, or money."

"Become a philanthropist."

"That's one idea. What else are you passionate about, Kensington?"

I shrugged. I did love to read, but didn't see anything worthwhile I could do in that regard.

"What about Whitby Press?"

"What of it?"

"With your love of reading, one would think working for such an esteemed publishing house would be very appealing."

"I never went to university."

"You sit on the board, do you not?"

"I forget how much you know about my life."

"What if you offered to review manuscript submissions or become an editorial assistant?"

"I'm not sure why you think they would offer me such a position."

"You will never know if you don't try. Besides, income wouldn't be a motivating factor for you."

"I would ring them up and say, what? 'Hello, may I please have something to read?'"

"It's a start."

It sounded absurd, but I appreciated Cortez's willingness to at least discuss my lack of purpose, so I'd hardly poopoo every idea he had.

His mobile vibrating startled me, and I sat up so he could reach over to get it. Instead of just looking at the screen, he stood and walked to the other side of the room.

"What is it?"

He met my gaze. "Arrangements have been made for me to meet with Otto von Habsburg."

"I see."

"I believe it's our best chance to figure out whether his cousin Konstantine still poses a threat to you."

"You believe Konstantine had something to do with Otto's attack?"

"I do."

"When?"

"Day after next."

"Which means?"

"We will have to cut our trip short. I'm sorry."

"It's only by a couple of days, Cortez. We stayed on far longer than I would've thought possible when we arrived."

When I approached and put my arms around him, he grasped the back of my neck with his hand and kissed me. "I hate the idea of giving up even a minute with you."

And I, him. But what would happen once this was all over? If he was able to determine I was no longer in danger, what would that mean? Would I then be allowed to return to my life and home in London?

Cortez's home was on the island of Mallorca. He lived his life globally because of his business.

I'd lost track of why he and I were together in the first place—because the Queen had engaged his services to protect me.

Once those services were no longer needed, what would happen between him and me?

The fact that he offered me no reassurances meant one of two things. He was either unaware of how I was feeling—which seemed hard to believe based on experience—or he knew my doubts and had nothing to quell them with.

22

Rile

I made every attempt to make our departure from the Seychelles as swift and easy as possible, without dwelling on the fact that we were cutting our trip short, particularly given we were only leaving two days earlier than planned. However, Kensington's mood as well as that of the rest of those who traveled with us was somber.

She did her best to hide her true feelings, but reading her like I was able to, I knew it wasn't just disappointment she was experiencing. She was worried, even fearful. She had every right to be.

Kensington knew as well as I did that there was more to what happened with Konstantine than sexual assault. He'd said that by the next night, he planned for them to be married. Showing up at King Ferdinand's palace had only reinforced the level of his obsession. While I didn't know exactly what role Otto played in all of this, my instincts told me it was significant.

Arranging where we'd meet was complex, and as it involved me asking a personal favor, it was something I had to do myself. The only people who could help me were my parents, and I had every intention of enlisting their aid.

I still believed Mallorca was the safest place for Kensington, and while I didn't question Angel's or Casper's abilities, I intended to keep Ink and Crash on her detail as well. Smoke and Siren would travel with me.

It took a full week after we arrived back in Mallorca to make all the arrangements for my meeting with not just Otto von Habsburg but his parents, Frederick and Wilhelmina, along with Konstantine and his father and mother, Karl and Maria.

Frederick and Karl were brothers. Otto was the eldest son of Frederick; Konstantine was Karl's. Decker dug deep into the Habsburg family, but found nothing that would indicate anything out of the ordinary in terms of the two sons' inheritance or that of their fathers.

I couldn't shake the feeling that was the key, but without Decker finding proof, I had nothing to go on.

The history of the Habsburgs was long and complicated, dating back to the 1020's construction of the castle from which they derived their name and which still stood in what was now Switzerland.

Between 1438 and 1765, the throne of the Holy Roman Empire was continuously occupied by the House of Habsburg. The family was able to vastly expand its domains to include Burgundy, Spain, and its colonial empire, Bohemia, Hungary, and other territories through a series of dynastic marriages.

As with most powerful empires, the house was eventually dissolved in 1806 due to an extinction in the male line. However, when a female descendant married into the House of Lorraine, that empire was soon renamed the House of Habsburg-Lorraine. The male heir from that union, dropped the lesser-known Lorraine and reverted the dynasty's name back to Habsburg. That branch of the family had ruled Austria until World War I.

Financially ruined, facing the threat of extinction in the male line a second time due to deaths in war and by illness, and powerful enemies in World War II, little was heard about the family to this day.

As Decker had said, the amount of inbreeding in order to keep their line "pure," had resulted in the opposite. I had no doubt there was some level of madness, perhaps evidence in each of the family members.

Even if I could get them to confess nothing, by having the six individuals who'd represented the once-powerful House of Habsburg in one room, I felt certain I could get enough information to know my next step.

The night before I was scheduled to leave Mallorca to travel first to Madrid and then on to London, I waited until I was certain Kensington was asleep before leaving the bed we shared to go to Celestina's gravesite. It had been so long since I felt her presence, and that troubled me. I hadn't seen her from a distance, but when I got closer to the small cemetery, I saw Marta placing a bouquet of flowers next to the headstone.

"I thought I might find you here tonight," I said as I approached and put my arm around her trembling shoulders.

"Today would have been her thirty-third birthday."

"Yes," I murmured. I hadn't forgotten, and never would. Marta had understood when I chose to only list the year of her daughter's birth and death on the marker since the day she was born and the day she died were the same, only twenty-six years apart.

We stood together silently for some time. Eventually, Marta left me alone. I sat on the cold grass and put my hand on the etched granite.

"Happy birthday, my love. I miss you so." I listened to the sound of the waves crashing on the shore, closed my eyes, and focused on how the breeze felt on my face.

It had been less than three months since I whisked Kensington away from the States, first to Mallorca, and then Madrid, and finally to the Seychelles. In that time, I had grown to care a great deal for her. She was beautiful and intriguing. Making love with her was better than it had been with anyone else ever, including my beloved Celestina. But I wondered, once this was all over, when Kensington was free to return to her home, live her life without a constant threat, would the magic I felt between us remain?

That the woman I'd married would've been thirty-three years old today, was a harsh reminder of Kensington's youth. In January, she had turned twenty-seven. In November, I had turned thirty-seven.

There were more than years between us; there were life experiences too innumerable to reflect on. It wasn't just losing my wife and unborn child that had aged me; the years of dangerous missions and the stress that went along with the life of an MI6 agent, compounded the wear on my body and my mind.

It was hard to admit, even to myself, that one of the reasons I left Her Majesty's Service and ventured out to form the Invincibles was that I was feeling the weight of my years.

The final straw for me had been the London subway and bus bombings. Witnessing the carnage the terrorists caused that day had been the impetus under which I contacted Decker and made him a partnership offer, followed by making the same one to Edge and Grinder.

When I walked into Z's office the day after learning over two hundred people were dead and thousands were injured, I'd already made up my mind to retire from active service.

"I'd hoped you'd take my place as chief one day, Rile," he'd said then. We both knew I never would have, whether the bombings happened or not.

I'd originally joined SIS because I believed every man and woman should be able to live their life free of tyranny, free of persecution, and free of fear. While my mother had been an agent before me, both she and my father lived their lives with the same purpose.

They were good people who, like my uncle, King Ferdinand, worked hard every day to ensure every person in Spain was afforded those freedoms.

Not everyone was born to the kind of life I led. Kensington certainly hadn't been. I didn't judge her for her upbringing or even her lack of a sense of purpose. I understood that she and I were on opposite ends of the spectrum in that regard. I'd known my purpose for many years and was ready to move into the next phase, one in which I slowed down, took on less, and relaxed more. In that way, I sounded like an old man. She, on the other hand, was a young woman, just beginning to figure out how she would make her mark on the world.

She'd been her grandparents' companion in the last years of their lives. I couldn't allow her to step into the same kind of role with me.

There would eventually come a day when she would want to spread her wings, and when that happened, she'd struggle with leaving me behind.

"You've made up your mind, haven't you?" came my beloved's beautiful voice.

I have. Allowing her to stay would be selfish. She deserves to make a full life for herself.

"You will break her heart, and yours too."

I shook my head. *Mine broke seven years ago, my darling. I was foolish to think it could ever mend.*

23

Kensington

It had been two hours since Cortez left the bed we shared and went to visit the grave of his deceased wife. If I were braver, I would've told him I was awake and that he didn't have to sneak away. I would always understand the need he had to spend time in the small cemetery. But there was something more to his visit to the grave tonight, and whatever it was, made him pull away from me.

I felt it the moment it happened, even though he was far enough away that I couldn't see him in the darkness. It was as though every cell in my body went stone cold. I felt abandoned, more alone than I'd ever felt in my life, even after my grandmother died.

The pain I felt was the same as when I watched her take her last breath and her hand went limp and cold in mine. The feeling of loss was so overwhelming then and now, that I hugged myself as silent sobs wracked my body.

Rather than wait for his return, I crept from the bed-room and took the stairs from the fifth level down to the fourth.

"Is everything okay?" Casper asked when I met her keeping watch on the landing.

I wiped away my tears and motioned with my hand toward the cemetery. "He needed time on his own."

Startling me, she put her hand on my shoulder. "I know how hard this is—today is the anniversary of her death."

I didn't think I could feel any worse pain, but Casper's words felt like a knife in my heart.

"You should go inside," she said, perhaps noticing me trembling.

I walked through the door and into the small bed-room that I knew was unoccupied. I fell onto the bed, buried my face in the pillow, and sobbed myself to sleep.

When I woke, the sun was high enough in the sky that I knew it was at least mid-morning. There was no sign that Cortez or anyone else had come looking for me. No doubt, there was someone keeping watch out-side my door.

Before we fell asleep last night, Cortez had told me he would be leaving first thing this morning. He didn't give me any details. He'd only said that upon his return, he hoped that Konstantine would no longer pose any kind of threat to me.

He didn't say anything about what would happen after that. We didn't talk about whether I'd stay on here with him or return to London. We didn't talk about whether we would still be together or if our love affair would end with his job to protect me.

Until he got up in the middle of the night and crept away, I was hopeful that we would still be together. Between then and now, the hope had vanished.

I felt like someone had died, but it wasn't a person; it was a relationship, or what I'd believed had been one.

"Kenzie?" I heard Teagon's voice followed by a knock on the door.

"Come in."

She closed the door behind her and sat on the edge of the bed. "Is everything okay?" she asked, just like Casper had when she saw me in the middle of the night.

I shook my head, crying too hard to answer. Teagon put her arms around me and held me as I dissolved back into tears.

24

Rile

When the plane landed and came to a stop on the tarmac of the private airfield in Madrid, I exited it only to walk several feet away and get on another plane, joined by Smoke and Siren.

Shortly after we were on board, a motorcade of black SUVs pulled up near the aircraft. I watched my parents get out of one and walk to the plane, followed by King Ferdinand and Queen Isabella along with their security.

"How are you, Cortez?" my mother asked, sitting beside me.

"I'm fine, Duchess, and you?"

My mother glared at me rather than answer.

The flight from Madrid to London was quick, a little less than two hours. When we landed, another motorcade was waiting on the tarmac, not far from where the pilot stopped the aircraft.

We deplaned in much the same order we'd arrived. The only difference was some of the King's security personnel remained behind after Smoke, Siren, and I exited.

We were whisked to Buckingham Palace without the same fanfare there might have been had this been an official state visit.

The SUVs pulled into an unmarked warehouse. From there, we'd drive through the tunnel that would take us to what I always referred to as the family entrance.

I sat and waited for the King, Queen, and my parents to exit their vehicle. Instead, the passenger door of the one I was riding in opened.

"Her Majesty has requested a private audience with you first, sir."

"Certainly." I followed the man inside and down an unfamiliar corridor. When he opened a door and motioned me inside, the Queen stood waiting.

"Your Majesty," I said, bowing.

She held her hand out to me. "The meeting that will be taking place is not the one you requested, Cortez."

"I see."

"I asked to speak with you first to suggest that you refrain from passing any kind of judgment until the meeting's end."

"Yes, ma'am."

"Thank you, Cortez. We'll join the others now." I followed her out a different door than the one through which I came in.

When we entered the room where I anticipated the meeting would be taking place, there was only one person present on behalf of the von Habsburgs—Karl, Konstantine's father.

Had the Queen not briefed me, I would have been livid. Respecting her wishes, I refrained from reacting until I heard what he had to say.

I stood off to the side and watched them go through the formalities. I took a seat only after everyone else had, everyone other than the security teams lining the room's edges—my own included.

"I would prefer to speak privately," Karl von Habsburg said directly to the Queen.

"We are."

He nodded and waited for her cue.

"You may tell the others what you told me."

He stood.

"What I am about to tell you is a closely guarded secret, until today." He cleared his throat. "As direct descendants of Emperor Karl I, the last Emperor of Austria, the last King of Hungary, the last King of Bohemia, and the last monarch belonging to the House of Habsburg before the dissolution of Austria-Hungary, we are bound by what is known as the Habsburg Family Statute."

His words validated my suspicion about Konstantine's motive. I didn't know how yet, but felt confident that by the end of his explanation, I would.

Karl von Habsburg went on to say that the edict, put in place in 1839, decreed that in order to "ensure the Habsburg dignity and serenity for now and forever," family members were only permitted to marry members of dynasties which had, at some point in history, reigned a sovereign nation. Furthermore, direct male descendants had to marry no later than the age of thirty.

The penalty of not doing both, was disinheritance and banishment from the family.

"The list of eligible families, as you can imagine, grows smaller with each generation. Slimmer still is the list of unmarried women of age from those families. In fact, there is only one—Francesca Alexandra Kensington Whitby."

And there it was. Every puzzle piece immediately fell into place. There were two heirs, both about to turn thirty, and only one woman to save either of them from banishment and disinheritance.

"Where is Konstantine now?" The Queen asked the very question on the tip of my tongue.

This was harder for the man; I could feel his tension and his sorrow.

"As you may have surmised, my son was, in fact, behind the attack on his cousin, believing that if Otto died, it would clear the way for him to be Miss Whitby's only suitor." Von Habsburg turned to me. "When you intervened in Budapest, my son believed you were kidnappers acting on behalf of his cousin."

He sat down, gripping the arms of the chair. "My son, as you also may have surmised, has suffered a mental breakdown. He has been institutionalized."

The Queen turned toward me and nodded.

"When was he committed?" I asked.

He took a deep breath. "After the attack on Otto, he was taken to an institution that did not have the same level of security as where he is now."

"You're saying he left the first facility and that is when he attempted to gain access to Miss Whitby while she was a guest in my home?" My uncle, like the Queen had earlier, asked the same question I had been about to ask.

"Yes, Your Majesty."

King Ferdinand, again like the Queen, turned to me and nodded.

"Where is your son presently?"

"Broadmoor Hospital."

I knew of it. It was a high-security psychiatric facility in Berkshire, England.

"In maximum security?"

He didn't immediately respond, filling me with dread.

"The family has made that request."

"And it has been denied?"

Von Habsburg nodded. "They disagree that it is necessary."

I wouldn't ask now, but the moment I was free to, I would find out exactly how to make it happen.

"How is Otto?" asked my mother when there was a lull in the conversation.

"He is quite well, actually. Thank you."

"What will become of the House of Habsburg if neither he nor Konstantine marry?" I asked.

"My brother and I are currently writing a stipulation into the statute. We are the only people with the authority to do so." Von Habsburg hung his head. "It is something we should've done years ago."

"How is your wife, Maria?" my mother asked.

"She is…not well."

"Her only child is suffering. I can only imagine how hard that must be on her."

There was something behind my mother's questions. Later, I would find out what exactly.

When the Queen stood, all others in the room did as well. She walked over to von Habsburg and took his hand. "I know how difficult this has been for you, Karl. I appreciate your honesty and willingness to share the plight of your family."

"Of course, Your Majesty," he responded, bowing.

The Queen turned to me. "Do you have any further questions, Cortez?"

"Not at this time, Your Majesty."

When she nodded, the two palace security team members standing closest to von Habsburg stepped forward and ushered him from the room. When the door closed behind them, the Queen took her seat.

"I have requested the prime minister look into the situation at Broadmoor. However, I cannot promise he will be able to sway the opinions of the doctors."

"Thank you, Your Majesty," I said.

When she invited us to stay on for that evening's dinner, I excused myself to make a call to Decker.

"Whoever you can get, I want on constant surveillance at Broadmoor Hospital. I don't want Konstantine von Habsburg as much as looking out the window."

"Roger that."

When I rang off, my first inclination was to call Kensington. It was a habit I had to break. Instead, I asked Smoke to brief Angel on what we'd learned this afternoon. "Do it with minimal detail," I told him. "Do not divulge the House of Habsburg Family Statute."

He responded the same way Decker had.

"Siren, you will be the point person for the team on hospital detail," I said when she turned to follow Smoke. "Make contact with Decker Ashford."

I stayed outside the room, attempting to compose myself before rejoining my family. What I learned today meant that Kensington was not in as much danger as we believed she had been. However, until I was certain Konstantine had been moved into maximum security, I wouldn't feel comfortable letting her go back to the way her life had been prior to her trip to Budapest. The decision wasn't entirely mine, though. It would be up to the Queen to determine the level of protection Kensington required moving forward.

I rubbed my chest where the pain sat, knowing I would soon say goodbye to the woman who had taken up temporary residence in my heart. My love for her would not end. Instead, it drove me to do what was best for her, and that did not include spending her life with me.

The door to the courtyard where I stood opened, and my mother joined me. She put her arms around me without speaking.

"I am sorry, Cortez. I wish you could see this differently."

"I cannot, Mother."

She cupped my cheek with her hand. "I feel your pain as if it were my own."

Rather than return to Madrid, I stayed on at the flat I kept in London. Like Kensington's, my residence was in the Knightsbridge neighborhood. The house she'd inherited from her grandparents was on Exhibition Road, steps from Hyde Park. My building was slightly farther away, closer to Brompton Oratory.

Unable to sleep, I rode the lift from the penthouse to street-level and walked the distance between the two; it was a little over a mile.

To think that all the years I lived in London, the beguiling woman who'd made me believe in love again was so close.

I continued walking until dawn, through the park, over to Kensington Gardens. I took the long way around back to my flat, returning just as the sun began to rise.

As much as I wanted to sleep, I couldn't. My pain sat too heavy on my chest. I closed my eyes, though, and imagined holding Kensington in my arms one last time—joining our bodies together in a way that I knew they never could be again.

25

Kensington

I woke with a start and sat up, confused by my surroundings. I'd been dreaming I was in the bed on the floor above, the one I'd once shared with Cortez, but never would again.

In my dream, his arms were around me. We kissed and came so close to making love that I nearly sobbed when my eyes opened and I was back in the small bedroom on the fourth floor.

More than our bodies being joined together, I missed the connection our souls shared. Unlike in my dream, awake, I could no longer feel the warmth of his love, and that broke my heart.

Knowing I wouldn't be able to fall back to sleep, I got out of bed, dressed, and took the outside stairs down to the first level. From there, I walked along the pathway that would lead to the chapel and cemetery. Like I had the first time, I sat down and traced the letters etched into the headstone with my fingertips.

I found some comfort, sitting here that I couldn't explain. It was as though being near the woman who Cortez would love forever, made me feel closer to him.

There were no questions for me to ask Celestina today. I was too afraid of the answers. I heard someone's footsteps on the gravel and looked up to see Teagon headed my way.

"Hey, Kenzie." She waited at the entrance to the small cemetery. I stood and walked over to her.

"Has something happened?"

"Let's go back to the house."

I put my hand on her arm. "Has something happened to Cortez?"

"No. I'm sorry if I worried you. Cortez is fine. There's news of Konstantine von Habsburg."

I followed her inside and sat at the table in the kitchen. Marta was there and poured me a cup of tea.

"As was suspected, Konstantine was behind the attack on his cousin."

I nodded.

"Apparently, he was committed to a psychiatric facility after it happened, but he was able to get out. That's when he came to Spain and attempted to get on the palace grounds. After that arrest, he was sent to another facility with more security."

"What happens now?"

"What do you want to do?"

"Go home?" It was a question rather than a statement. I truly did want to go back to not being under someone's constant scrutiny, but going home meant my time with Cortez would come to an end. The truth I had to face was that he didn't want me here anyway. It would be far better if I left on my own rather than wait for him to tell me to. I covered my face when my eyes filled with tears.

"Kenz?"

"I need to make a call. Can you excuse me, please?" Considering I almost never called my great-aunt, I hoped she wouldn't see my doing so now as a terrible intrusion.

When I rang off several minutes later, I'd gotten the answer I wanted, but I wasn't any happier. I was going to miss Cortez more than I could admit. Going back to London was the last thing I wanted to do, but I knew it was for the best.

"I've received permission to return home," I told Teagon when I found her waiting in the other room.

"Do I need to ask from whom?"

"Someone with more authority than Cortez or even your boss."

"Got it. When would you like to leave?"

"As soon as possible."

"Very well. I'll make the arrangements."

"No, I will."

26

Rile

"What do you mean Kensington is gone?" I asked when Ink told me she, Angel, and Casper had left Mallorca. "I never authorized this."

"Smoke briefed Angel directly. When she asked me to take them to the airport, I had no reason to think she hadn't cleared it with either him or you."

I was pacing back and forth in my office, wondering how, in such a short amount of time, things had gone straight to hell. Never once had I said that they should leave Spain. Never once had I said that Kensington shouldn't remain under full protection. "Who arranged their travel?"

"Angel?"

"Is that a bloody question, Ink?"

"Look, Rile, I know you're pissed, but I'll repeat what I said earlier. Smoke briefed Angel directly. Angel. Who has been on Kensington's detail longer than the rest of us. She and Casper told me they were leaving to return to London. Are you seriously suggesting I should've contacted you to confirm? Cause I gotta tell you, Rile, both of them would've had my balls if I had."

"I've another call to make." I rang off and called Smoke, who I lit into worse than I had Ink. "I told you to brief Angel. Not call off the fucking op."

"I did exactly what you told me to do."

"Where in the name of God did Angel get the idea that they could leave Mallorca?" I felt as though all I was doing was repeating myself and not getting a single answer.

"Hey, Rile, why don't you ask *her*?"

"I haven't been able to reach her." Or Kensington or Casper. "If you hear from any of the three of them, tell them to get in touch with me immediately."

I ended that call and rang Decker. "I need to know how in the hell they're traveling," I said after explaining the situation.

"Get right back to you."

I tried each of the women again while I waited; each call went straight to voicemail. I rang Ink back. "Where's Crash?"

"Right here."

When I growled, I heard the mobile rustle.

"Hey, Rile. Look, I'm sorry about this. Neither Ink nor I had any idea that Angel was operating outside of direct orders."

"Where in the hell are they, Crash?"

"On their way to London. Didn't Ink tell you that?"

"Do you have any idea what airline, when they took off, when they're scheduled to arrive?"

"No, but I think I can find out."

"Please do."

Between Decker and him, I hoped one of them could tell me something. I was still pacing when I heard the elevator that opened directly into the foyer of the penthouse. The last person I expected to see walk out of it, did. "Kensington?"

"May I come in?"

"Of course." I stepped aside and then looked behind her.

"They're waiting downstairs."

"I see. I'm surprised by your arrival. Your departure from Mallorca was premature."

"I heard Konstantine is in a psychiatric facility. Is that untrue?"

"He is in a facility, but not with the level of security we'd prefer before having you return to London."

"I'm happy to be home. Going home, anyway. We stopped here first."

"I'm glad you did. I've been worried."

She turned her back to me and put her hands in the pockets of jeans I'd never seen her wear. In fact, I wondered where she got them.

"I want to thank you for everything you did to keep me safe, Rile. I've already spoken with the Queen and have given you an excellent report." She turned to me with a ridiculously fake smile pasted on her face.

I now knew where she'd gotten permission to leave Mallorca. I would have to tread lightly with the Queen if I chose to address it at all. Her use of my code name, though, rankled. "Kensington…stop this."

"Look, I only came to say goodbye. So, again, thanks." She stuck her hand out as if I would consider shaking it. I didn't.

"We need to talk, my darling."

The look on her face changed to a scowl that better conveyed her current mood. "Don't call me that."

"Can I get you a drink? A glass of wine perhaps?"

"No, thank you. I won't be staying."

When I took a step forward, she took a step back and then turned away from me a second time. "You could have at least had the decency to end it, Cortez. Not just pretend that nothing ever happened between us."

I walked closer and put my hands on her shoulders. I wouldn't tell her she was jumping to the wrong conclusion. I wouldn't tell her she was wrong about things ending between us, because she wasn't. "I had every intention that we'd talk."

"When?"

"When I returned to Mallorca."

"And when was that to be?"

"Once I was certain that Konstantine was under lock and key."

"You left without a word."

"It was very early. I didn't want to disturb you."

She jerked out from under my hands that were still on her shoulders, and walked to the other side of the room. "That's bloody bullshit, and you know it. You left our bed without a word. You left Mallorca without a word. You left *me,* Cortez, without a word." Her eyes filled with tears.

"Kensington, you and I both know—"

"Don't!" she shouted. "Don't say that I know anything. If you want to speak, speak for yourself, but don't you dare speak for me."

Everything I considered saying sounded trite, even to myself. I took a deep breath and let it out slowly. "I wish we were at the same place in life, but we are not."

"Is this how it goes with all of them? Do you seduce all the women under your protection? Pretend that what the two of you have is something special? Get them to fall in love with you? And then, when the job is finished, you walk away before they know what hit them."

You know none of that is true.

I saw her flinch and then close her eyes. She felt my words. What would she do? Would she acknowledge them?

She rolled her shoulders and folded her arms. "I've got to hand it to you, you've got it down to a science."

I watched as she walked over and picked up a bag. I'd been too overjoyed to see her that I hadn't noticed it when she set it on the chair.

"I'm returning this to you, Cortez."

"What is it?" I asked when she tried to hand me the bag, even though I didn't need to know.

"The Miró. I can't keep it."

"I want you to have it. It was—it is—a gift, Kensington."

"Given under false pretenses." She set the bag on the kitchen counter. *I don't want it, Cortez, just like you don't want me.*

I couldn't tell her she was wrong, that I did want her, more than anyone I'd ever wanted. "I want you to have a full and happy life, Kensington." I took the painting from the bag, unwrapped it, and pointed to the shape of the female. "This is the woman you deserve to be. Happy. Joyous. I know you will find the man who makes you feel this way. He's the man you deserve to be with." *I cannot be that man. I don't have it in me anymore.*

Kensington studied me for several seconds. I longed to know what she was thinking, but she was no longer giving anything away.

She stepped closer, leaned forward, and kissed my cheek. "Goodbye, Cortez."

When Kensington walked out of the foyer and over to the elevator that seemed to open at her silent command, I didn't follow. If I had, I would've begged her to stay with me forever.

27

Kensington

The first two days after I returned to London, I spent mostly crying. And then I stopped. Two days after that, I told Casper I no longer required her services.

She looked between Teagon and me. "I need to check in with Rile."

"I'll take care of it," said Teagon when Casper left the room.

I knew I'd have to say the same to my best friend one day very soon, but I wasn't ready. Every day, I prayed she wouldn't come to me to say she'd been given another mission.

A few minutes later, Teagon walked into the kitchen where I was rummaging in the fridge for something to eat and missing the hell out of Marta.

"She's gone."

I closed the fridge and spun around. "What? She left? Just like that?"

"Isn't that what you wanted?"

I shrugged. "Yes, but, what is it with you MI6-types? Do you always leave without as much as a goodbye?"

"Nah. She's CIA. Or was once."

I reached for the bottle of wine I'd opened the night before and poured a glass. "Fancy some?"

"I best not. On duty and all that."

"About that."

"Go on."

"Who employs you?"

"MI6, as you well know."

"To whom do you answer?"

"Presently, the chief, Z Alexander."

"Am I still, officially, under protection?"

"You are, Kenzie."

"For how long?"

She shrugged and grabbed the bottle of wine. "What the hell. One glass won't hurt."

"Teagon, for how long?"

"Until we're absolutely certain that Konstantine is no longer a threat."

"How long might that be?"

"I'm sorry, Kenz. I don't know."

"You can't stay on here forever. Gawd, you'd have the most boring life known to man."

She took a drink of wine, set her glass down, and folded her arms in front of her. "Um, no. That would be your life, my friend."

"What? How's that fair? I've been under fucking house arrest for months."

"What of it? What's next, Kenz?"

I took a big gulp of wine and poured what was left in the bottle into my glass. "I'm no longer sharing with you."

"I didn't want more anyway."

"So what do you think I should be doing?"

"What do you want to do?"

I'd tell her I didn't know, but that would be a lie. Since we returned to London, I'd been thinking about some of the suggestions Cortez made. Two things in particular. First, the notion of me working for Whitby Press, even if only as a volunteer. The second was, which of the charities my grandparents supported did I want to get more involved with?

"I do have some ideas."

When she said, "You're joking." I wanted to smack her.

"It was something you-know-who and I talked about."

"The man whose name shall forever go unmentioned?"

"Correct. Anyway, *he* suggested that I consider seeking a position with Whitby Press."

"That's a fantastic idea!"

"Is it? Why?"

"Gawd, Kenz, you own the bloody place. March in there and tell them you're taking over."

"Very funny."

"What? I'm not kidding. I just said I thought it was a fantastic idea."

"I never went to university. I can't just go plop myself down and run a business I know nothing about."

"Then go and learn. They all work for you, Kenz. Schedule a meeting with whomever's running the place now and tell him or her that you want to start working in some capacity."

"That ought to go over well."

"Why not?"

"Bored family member comes in and demands a job. Come on, be serious."

"What do you think Whit did?"

"What do you mean? What about my father?"

"Who do you think publishes all those bloody photography books of his?"

I hadn't really thought about it, but Whitby Press did. "He's talented."

"Not *that* talented."

"They must make money, or they wouldn't do it."

"Right." She shook her head.

"Are you saying they lose money on my father's books? I'm sure someone would've said so in one of the board meetings."

She shook her head a second time. "They have plenty of other books that make up for it, I'm sure. Could you imagine, Kenz? 'Oh, by the way, Miss Whitby, so glad you could join us today so we could talk to you about how long your father's books have been bleeding us dry.' Seriously, what do you think?"

I didn't know what to think, but I certainly planned to look into it.

"Besides, you read more than anyone I know. Anyone I've ever known."

I would confess to being a voracious reader. Always had been. As an only child, it gave me something to do. Plus, Gran Bea always had a book going. "I do enjoy reading very much."

"See? Call them tomorrow. Now, what are your other ideas?"

"What do you mean?"

"You said 'some ideas.' What are the others?"

"The others weren't for jobs per se."

"So?"

"I've been thinking of getting more involved in some charities. I was so moved by the visit to the hospital in Madrid Christmas night, weren't you?"

Teagon smiled but didn't comment.

"What now?"

"I'm proud of you, Kenz. You're a grown-up."

"Sod off."

"Don't take offense. I'm serious."

"That until now I've been a child?"

"That until now you hadn't found your way."

"That's what Gran Bea used to say."

Teagon shrugged. "Great minds and all that."

"More wine?" Maybe I could share after all.

"Nah, better not. I need to go out and give the guys the new schedule."

"What?"

"Oh, come on, Kenz. You really didn't think that it was you, Casper, and me all alone since we've been here. Z added to your detail shortly after we arrived back in London."

"Who else is here?"

"No one from Rile's team, if that's what you're thinking."

"Who, then?"

"MI5."

"How many?"

"Just two, but soon to be three."

I rolled my eyes. "Just two, but soon to be three. This is bloody ridiculous. I'm not this important."

Teagon stood when I did and hugged me. "You're far more important than you realize, Kensington Whitby."

"Why did you ask Casper to leave if you knew Z would add another person from MI5?"

"Because it's what you wanted, Kenz. Look, I understand. She works for Rile. Her being here was a connection to him. Honestly, it was time she left anyway. Best that your detail is handled solely by SIS now."

I went upstairs and attempted to power up my lap-top. First, I had to find the cord. I had no idea the last time I'd used it.

After the computer finally came on and I'd sorted through the first few of thousands of emails, I searched for the most recent communications I'd received from Whitby Press.

I opened one of the financial reports and groaned when I saw it was over one hundred pages. I skimmed the first few, didn't understand a single thing I'd read, and decided that should be my first request—that someone explain the damn things to me.

In the meantime, I went to one of the more popular online booksellers and searched my father's name. Good Lord! My dad, Michael Alexander Whitby, had more than thirty books for sale online. I scrolled through the most popular ones and bit my bottom lip. Even without understanding the quarterly financial reports of Whitby Press, I could figure out that if his most popular book was ranked above a million on the bestseller list, he probably didn't sell even one book a month.

The next morning, I did as Teagon suggested and rang Whitby Press to ask for a meeting. I was shocked when, after asking me to hold for a moment and before I'd even explained my reason for calling, I was transferred to none other than the managing director himself—a man who had only recently been promoted to the position and who was highly qualified despite his young age.

"Kensington, this is Lincoln Mulrooney. What a delight to hear from you."

I explained the reason for my call, saying that I had a few questions about the latest reports and also wished to meet with someone regarding potential job openings.

"My day is quite booked, but what about this evening? We could meet for dinner at Five Hertford at, say, eight?"

"I don't want to disturb you in the evening, Mr. Mulrooney. Tomorrow would be fine. Or another day this week."

"My days are typically tightly scheduled. It would be far easier if we were to meet after."

Asking how he was able to finagle a membership at the exclusive Five Hertford club would make me sound like a bloody snob, but I couldn't help but wonder how he had.

"You'd be pleased to know that I'm having dinner this evening with Whitby Press' managing director,"

I told Teagon when I came downstairs in search of breakfast.

"Linc Mulrooney?"

"Linc? First name basis with him, are you?"

"It's commonly known that's what he goes by."

"What else do you know about him?"

"He's hot as fuck. Smart as all bloody hell."

"Nice language, Teag."

"Since when are you, of all people, such a prude?"

"What do you mean?"

"Nothing. Never mind."

"No. You called me out. I want to know why."

"I was wrong. Stupid thing to say." When her cheeks flushed red, I knew that whatever she was referring to had something to do with Cortez. So, yes, I'd drop it.

"We're meeting at Five Hertford."

Her eyebrows went up practically to her hairline.

"That's what I thought. I know it makes me sound awful, but what's his connection?"

"I'll see what I can find out, but whatever it is, must be a closely guarded secret or I'd already know."

I'd never had any secrets from Teagon, but the idea that Cortez or any of her other colleagues knew everything about me, pissed me off. Not that I could do anything about it. I was connected to the Queen, and my life had always been an open book—to SIS anyway.

"What time are you meeting?"

"Eight."

Teagon said she'd make the necessary security arrangements for my meeting with Mulrooney. However, neither she nor any of the other security people would be permitted entrance to the club. Perhaps if the Queen herself was dining there, her team would be permitted entrance, but she'd never put herself or the other members of Five Hertford through that sort of thing.

I hadn't been to the club since my grandfather passed away. My eyes filled with tears when I walked through the unmarked door after the *maître d'* opened it.

"Miss Whitby, it is such a pleasure to see you again." The man and I cheek-kissed. "We miss your grandparents very much."

Not more than I. "Thank you, Ford."

"I believe you're meeting Mr. Mulrooney. He'll be waiting in the lounge, Miss."

I thanked him again and followed him to the spiral staircase that would take me downstairs. I would typically avert my eyes when walking past the various dining rooms, but when a familiar feeling came over me, I couldn't help but look. In the corner, sat Cortez with a strikingly beautiful woman I didn't recognize. He was so enthralled by whatever she was saying, he didn't look up and see me.

"I've a request that we not be seated in the library this evening. I wouldn't normally make a fuss, but in this case, I'd consider it a personal favor if you'd arrange for us to sit elsewhere."

"Yes, Miss Whitby."

I knew from his response that the library was exactly where our table had been reserved. I couldn't possibly sit in the same room with Cortez and another woman. If there was no other option, I'd be forced to feign illness and leave.

Lincoln Mulrooney stood when he saw me approach. "You look lovely, Kensington."

"Thank you."

"I took the liberty," he said, handing me a glass of wine. I took a sip and recognized it immediately as one of my favorites. It was exactly what I would've ordered for myself. "I was pleased to receive your call earlier," he said, leading me to a table and pulling out a chair for me.

"You may not be when you learn what I'd like to discuss."

"You said you had questions about the reports you receive?"

"Yes, but it was my other reason for calling that you may find harder to address."

"About working for Whitby Press? Not in the least. Speaking for myself along with the rest of the management team as well as the members of the board, we'd be delighted to have you on staff, in whatever capacity you desire."

"Why?"

He set his glass of wine on the table and leaned forward.

"Why, indeed. I pose the same question to you."

"But you didn't answer mine."

"I only had the pleasure of meeting your grandfather one time. However, he did little besides extol your virtues. Whitby Press could only benefit from your direct involvement."

"As it does my father's?"

He laughed. "It is with the deepest respect for his talent that we continue to publish your father's work."

"Would there ever come a time when you'd refuse to do so?"

He smiled at me with warm brown eyes, and my heart nearly melted. Teagon was right. Mr. Mulrooney was hot as fuck. He would be the perfect model on the covers of the books Whitby published, at least in the romance genre. He would also serve as an outstanding example for any non-fiction book about the world's most handsome man, or how to work twelve hours a day and maintain a bodybuilder's physique.

His hair and beard were salt and pepper, belying his age. I couldn't remember exactly how old he was, other than being surprised when someone quoted it to me.

"I'd give anything to know what you're thinking right now."

"You're ridiculously handsome," I said without apology. It wasn't a compliment; it was a statement of fact.

"Thank you, Kensington. I feel that opens things up for me to very unprofessionally tell you, you are the single most-attractive woman I've ever laid eyes on."

"Thank you." After seeing Cortez upstairs, my bruised heart and ego were soothed by Lincoln's praise.

He cleared his throat. "While having dinner for the sake of enjoying your company would be exceedingly pleasurable, you did have things you wished to discuss."

"My apologies for—"

He rested his hand on mine. "Please, no apologies, Kensington, about anything."

"Excuse me, Mr. Mulrooney, Miss Whitby, your table is ready whenever you are," said Ford when he approached our table.

"Shall we?"

Ford cleared his throat. "Sir, a change in rooms has been necessitated. I hope there is no inconvenience."

"None at all," he responded, but I could see faint lines etched in his forehead.

"It was per my request," I explained.

He nodded and put his hand on the small of my back as we followed Ford up the stairs, past the library, and to the most private of Five Hertford's dining rooms.

"Allow me," Lincoln said before Ford could help me with my chair. "I much prefer this room. Thank you," he leaned forward and whispered.

Once we were alone, I felt it only fair I explain why I'd made the request. "There was someone seated in the library…"

He smiled and rested his hand on mine a second time. "Say no more. I'll consider it my good fortune."

28

Rile

The very moment Kensington entered the building, I felt her presence. I would have regardless of whether I had been expecting her or not.

"Is that the woman everyone in the family has been talking about?" asked my cousin Serena.

"Yes. Also the one I told you about earlier." Serena had asked me to join her for dinner this evening, but after I received word that Kensington would be here, I explained to my cousin why I was changing the venue.

"She's lovely."

My cousin and I returned to our discussion about her impending divorce, the reason she'd asked me to dinner, and what she was requesting from me.

"I would do anything for you, Serena. You know this. However, looking deeper into your husband's infidelity will only serve one purpose, and that will be to hurt you."

"I have to know, Cortez."

"Why? Your prenuptial agreement ensures he won't get a penny of your money." I scrubbed my face with my hand, wishing I had a better argument to talk her out of what she was asking. "Go out and find your own happiness instead. Knowing will only make you bitter."

"It looks as though she's finding her own happiness as well." My cousin motioned with her head toward the hallway where Kensington was being escorted to a different dining room by Lincoln Mulrooney, the managing director of Whitby Press.

Evidently, she'd seen me when she came in. That would be the only explanation for the change in dining rooms.

"What about finding your own happiness, Cort? How will you do that when you are so in love with her?"

I brushed my lower lip with my fingertip. I could feel Kensington's pain, and it was my fault. What had I been thinking by showing up here tonight? The only thing I'd achieved was add to the sorrow Kensington and I were both already feeling.

My cousin was, thankfully, the most talkative person in our family, so we didn't suffer through awkward silence while my mind was elsewhere.

In the same way I knew when she arrived, I also knew when Kensington left.

"Shall we?" I said a few minutes later.

Serena reached across the table and covered my hand with hers. "Cortez, as much as you don't want to see me hurt, I don't want you to be either. Tell this woman how you feel about her. I know you will be happy you did. So will she."

I was in the midst of a workout the next day when I received a call from Grinder.

"Hello, my friend. I assume all is well with you and Pia?"

"You don't have to assume, Rile," he laughed. "You know they are. You probably also know the reason for my call."

"Enlighten me."

When Grinder asked me to stand beside him as his best man, I was overcome with unexpected emotion. "I would be proud, my friend."

"Neither of us is good at this kind of conversation. Actually, you probably are, but I'm not. However, it's important to me that you know why I'm asking."

He paused, but I was too choked up to speak.

"You're the one who convinced me I could be this happy, Rile. If you hadn't been your typical bloody blunt self, I may never have had the courage to face my demons head-on, but more importantly, to share them with the woman I love so that, together, we could overcome them. Not mine, but hers too. Thank you, Rile. I know Pia shares my appreciation for you and reveres you in the same way I do."

"You would have found your way with or without my influence. You and Pia are meant to be together. You have been since the day you met."

It was on a summer holiday with his parents when my friend and business partner had met the woman who would soon be his wife. They'd both been sixteen at the time, and while life had handed them each more than their share of tragedies, the fact that they were together and happy was all that mattered now.

"When is the wedding?"

"The first week of May."

29

Kensington

The first week I spent at Whitby Press was equally exhausting and exhilarating. Linc arranged for a desk to be added to his office, and every day for the last month, he and I had worked side by side as I learned about the publishing house that had been in my family for generations.

I still had no idea what he saw in me that made him believe I was cut out to work here, but he spent enough time praising and reassuring me over the course of the last six weeks that, little by little, I stopped doubting myself.

After our dinner at Five Hertford, we both backed off of anything flirtatious, and I was grateful. I still found him attractive, but I wasn't attracted to him. I wondered if it was too soon after Cortez, or if I'd always feel that no man who could ever take his place in my heart.

It wasn't into Whitby Press alone that I'd thrown myself in order to keep my mind off the man who had broken my heart. I'd also become a volunteer at Great Ormond Street Hospital for children. Known to most as GOSH, the almost-two-hundred-year-old facility was one of the world's leading childhood disease research centers.

As Cortez had suggested, I found the thing I was best at was offering support to the parents of children in hospital, the mothers in particular.

While I'd suggested to Teagon that she could resign her position as my personal bodyguard, she was intransigent that, when that time came, it would be her boss who instructed her to do so. She promised she wasn't going mad with boredom since I spent all my time either in the office or at the hospital.

While being so busy kept me from thinking of Cortez every minute of the day, the pain of missing him was ever-present.

"What do you say we take a break for lunch today?" Linc suggested.

"Do we have time?"

He smiled. "With you doing half my work, I wonder if I might have my hours and salary cut."

"Ha, ha." I spent the majority of my time reading. Sometimes it was manuscripts, but I usually took those home with me at night. The rest of the time, it was marketing and financial reports. Little by little, I was learning about every genre of book we published and what the profit margins were within each.

Art books, the category in which my father's books fell, was the least profitable of all. However, it was a market segment we'd never pull back from. The board believed it was important we continue to bring art to the masses in any way we could.

My reading preference had always been and remained fiction. Mystery and suspense more than any other genre, so I was thrilled when I was able to take home a manuscript that had been sent up for consideration. I stared longingly at the one I had sitting on my desk, but a girl had to eat too.

"Sure, lunch sounds great." I sent a text to Teagon to let her know to tell whoever was on my detail this afternoon that I'd be going out.

"Where to?" I asked when we left the building.

"How's Greek sound?"

"Brilliant."

"Shall we walk?"

"Equally brilliant." We hadn't gotten very far when who should I see but Cortez, running toward us? I veered off the path, stood next to a tree, and turned my back.

"Kensington? Is everything okay?"

"Yes…um…fine." Gawd, why couldn't I think of a single reason why I'd suddenly taken an abrupt and ridiculous turn into the woods?

Linc walked around me so he faced me. "Do you want to explain?"

"No."

He looked over my shoulder. "Is the man you're avoiding about my height, bald?"

"Yes."

"Then, I'm afraid we're going to be here quite a while."

"Why?"

"Because he's standing on the path, hands on hips, doing what I can only assume is waiting for you." Linc cleared his throat. "Correction, he's coming this way."

"Would you mind excusing us?" I heard Cortez say.

When Linc looked into my eyes questioningly, I nodded.

"I'll just be out…you know…there." He waved his hand in the direction of the path.

"Kensington?"

"What?" I said without turning around.

"Would you please look at me?"

"No."

"What you're doing now isn't safe."

I spun around and folded my arms. "Why are you in London?"

"I have a home in London."

"Nowhere near as nice as your home in Mallorca."

He raised a brow.

"Nothing is as nice as that house."

He smiled. "Thank you."

Being this close to him was hell. Absolute hell. I longed to wrap my arms around him like I used to, have him run his fingers through my hair, and kiss me.

"Kensington."

"Please, I beg you, don't look at me like that."

"Like what?"

"Like you know exactly what I'm thinking."

His eyes softened. "It makes it very difficult for your security team to keep you safe when you run into the woods."

"What do you know of my security team?"

"Your safety will always be important to me, Kensington." He looked over his shoulder. "Are you seeing him?"

"That's none of your business."

He nodded and slowly closed his eyes and then opened them. I could feel his pain as well as my own.

"That's Lincoln Mulrooney, managing director of Whitby Press and my boss, of sorts."

Cortez smiled. "I'm happy for you."

I couldn't read the look on his face. "I'm surprised you didn't know." I walked out to the pathway and over to Linc. "You might want to head on without me."

"You're sure?"

"Sorry about lunch. I'll make it up to you."

"You're sure you're all right?"

"I'm fine. Old friend."

Once Linc left, I turned back toward Cortez. "I'm not seeing him. I'm working at Whitby Press."

He motioned to a nearby bench. "I saw you with him at Five Hertford."

"I saw you too," I spat.

"With my cousin Serena. She's going through a divorce and wanted me to use some of my skills to make her soon-to-be-ex husband's life a living hell."

I laughed. "Was it a coincidence that you were there?"

"No."

I was back to being annoyed with him. "Who told you?"

"I get briefings."

"From?"

"You're not going to like the answer."

"Teagon?" I gasped.

"No. Not exactly."

"One of the other guys?"

"I'm copied on the reports that go to Z."

"Is Teagon aware of this?" Now I was angry.

"She is not, and that was Z's decision."

"She'll be as furious as I am."

"It will continue to happen whether she's aware of it or not."

Something occurred to me. "How often do you get these reports?"

"Sometimes twice a day, why?"

"Is that why you're here now? You knew Linc and I were going to lunch?"

"No. That was an honest coincidence. I did plan to contact you today, though."

I folded my arms and looked away from him. "Why?"

"I have to go out of town."

His words pained me. Why should I know whether he was in or out of town? When he put his hand on my arm, I jerked it away.

"I realize you got approval from the Queen before returning to London. I have little recourse in that regard if I want to remain in her good graces. However, if it had been up to me, you would still be on Mallorca."

"And you would be here in London?"

"Not necessarily, no."

My head began to ache. Had I made a terrible mistake by leaving too soon? I turned back toward him. *"Do not read my thoughts!"*

He smiled. "I've told you time and again that it doesn't always work that way, Kensington. Especially if you don't want me to know what you're thinking."

"What if I'm too late, and I think it before I realize I don't want you to know?"

He leaned into me so our arms were touching. It made me want to crawl into his lap and kiss him.

"You know what it's like when your emotions are moving faster than your thoughts. It's the same for me. You affect me as much as I do you, my darling. I cannot always think clearly in your presence."

"Don't call me that," I whispered.

"I'm sorry. There are times I can't help it."

"Why would I still be on Mallorca?"

He sighed. "Because I'm not certain Konstantine has been effectively neutralized."

"Is that the only reason?"

He grasped my hand, and this time, I didn't jerk it away. "I care very much for you, Kensington. So much so, that I would break my own heart first rather than allow you to live a life that would ultimately make you unhappy."

"Being with you wouldn't make me unhappy."

"Maybe not right away. Eventually, you would be, though."

"How can you be so certain? Can you also see into the future?"

"I am far older than you, my dear. I am set in my ways. I travel for work far too often."

I rolled my eyes. "You're not that old, Cortez."

"Perhaps not in years, but in spirit."

"I'm not the right woman for you."

"What makes you say it that way?"

"You'd do anything for the right woman. If you loved her and wanted her in your life, you'd do anything to make it happen." While the pain didn't lessen, the realization that it was as simple as that, seemed to help me accept that Cortez and I would never be together. I removed my hand from his. "Where are you going? Can you say?"

His eyes scrunched, perhaps at my abrupt change of subject. "To Italy. Grinder is getting married."

"That's wonderful. Please give him my regards for much happiness." I stood, suddenly famished. "I must get back to work."

"I'll walk with you."

"Is that really necessary?" I looked around the park. "I can't see them, but I'm sure my guard dogs are in close proximity."

"Allow me to anyway?"

I shook my head. "It's best if you don't. I understand, Cortez, I truly do. But my heart hasn't quite caught up with my head just yet."

When I returned to the office, Linc wasn't there, but on my desk sat a Greek salad and grilled pita bread. It was exactly what I would have ordered.

I wasn't ready to think about getting involved with another man, and for now, Linc and I worked together. In the long run, being romantically involved might make things very awkward. However, when I was ready to move on, he was just the kind of man I'd do it with.

30

Rile

Between the time I said goodbye to Kensington and left Hyde Park, and this morning, I'd been filled with a sense of dread. Perhaps it was the finality I felt when she and I said goodbye.

Kensington was wrong. She was the right woman. I loved her, and like Celestina, I'd love her until the day I died. Because of that love, I couldn't ask her to give up so much of her life for me.

She looked different to me yesterday. Fulfilled, I suppose. She'd taken her life by the reins and was living it. It was what I'd wanted for her, and London was the perfect place for her to do it. Eventually, once I was certain Konstantine was no longer a threat, I would return to Mallorca. Maybe I'd even sell my London flat. I could easily stay in one of MI6's apartments if Z hired the Invincibles for a mission necessitating my being here. I could also stay in a hotel.

Rather than focusing on my sorrow and unease, I needed to direct my thoughts to Grinder and Pia. I rang my driver and grabbed my bag. Once at the airfield, my flight to Florence would take a little over an hour.

***

The small chapel on the grounds of *Antica Cascina dei Conti di Valentini,* the estate and winery that had been in the family of Grinder's soon-to-be wife for generations, was filled to capacity. Love reverberated from its walls and through every person seated in it.

"How are you, my friend?" I asked, putting my hand on Grinder's shoulder.

"Never better."

"You deserve this and every happiness," I said, brushing a tear away. Was it for that happiness that I was crying, or was it because I'd never know it to this extent again?

When the music began to play, I looked to the back of the chapel and watched the two bridesmaids walk to where we stood. The music changed, those in the pews stood, and Grinder's fiancée, Pia, began her walk toward us. Although, she didn't walk at all. She danced her way down the aisle. Love and happiness seeped from her every pore, and her eyes stayed fixed on those of my friend.

I couldn't help but think of Kensington and the joy I wouldn't be there to witness on the day she wed. As hard as I tried to keep my focus on the man and woman about to be married, I couldn't stop thinking about her. Instead of thinking about Celestina and the way she'd looked on our wedding day, I could only see Kensington in my mind. What she'd wear. The flowers she'd carry. Even where she would be married. It felt like a knife in my chest when I realized what I was picturing was the tiny chapel on my own estate on Mallorca.

The harder I tried to close my mind to the images flashing before it, the faster they came. Not just the wedding, but the birth of Kensington's first child, of her holding the tiny boy in her arms and beaming up at the father. Then of her playing in the sand on the steps below my house, with her children. She had four, just like she'd said. Why was my own mind torturing me this way?

I could hear the words of the priest as he led Grinder and Pia through their vows, but it was as if my ears were stuffed with cotton. The only words I could hear clearly were those spoken by Kensington in my imagination. I could hear her talking to her children, telling them how much she and their daddy loved them.

When I heard the priest ask us to bow our heads in prayer, I didn't pray along with him. I prayed to God to please stop torturing me this way. I wanted nothing more than to be joyous for my friend and his wife, not mired down in my own unhappiness.

God refused to answer my prayers. For the rest of the night, I was plagued by visions of Kensington. No matter how hard I tried to distract myself in conversation with the other wedding guests, a reel of Kensington's life without me continued to play in the back of my mind.

"Is everything okay?" Grinder asked shortly before it was time for the couple to depart the reception.

"Never better, my friend. My heart overflows with happiness for you."

Pia came and stood beside him, wrapping her arm through his. "Thank you, Rile," she said, leaning forward to kiss my cheek. "Thank you for making sure he found his way back to me."

"The two of you were always meant to be together, sweet Pia."

"I hope you find that too," she said.

I bid them goodnight, and once they'd said their long goodbyes to their other guests and were gone, I drove back to Florence and spent the night in a hotel close to the airfield.

My dreams, like every minute at the wedding, were filled with Kensington at every stage of her life without me. I woke with tears streaming down my cheeks, wondering if I would be cursed by the madness of not being able to escape witnessing her happiness from afar.

When I woke the next morning, the visions were gone. In their place, I felt Celestina. She didn't speak to me, but I could feel her calming presence.

When I boarded my plane an hour later, I suddenly felt a chill. *Celestina? Please don't leave me,* I begged.

"Cortez, my love…"

Don't go, I begged again. I feared that without her, the visions of Kensington would return. I couldn't bear the pain of it. It would be easier to allow the pain of missing my beloved wife to claw its way back into my soul. That pain I knew. I was accustomed to it. It wasn't new and raw like that which had entered my heart with the realization that Kensington would one day marry another man, have children with him, be happy. It's what I wanted for her, but never did I imagine the pain would be more excruciating than anything I'd ever felt before.

My eyes fill with tears as I murmured, "Celestina." *Please, I beg you, come back to me. You were more than my northern star. You were my sun, my moon, my universe, my guiding light. Without you, I'm lost. So lost.*

When I heard the chimes indicating our descent, I forced myself to look out the plane's window, below to Mallorca, the island that I'd made my home. Where my beloved and our unborn child were buried. The house, my house, was not destined to echo the happy sounds of my children running through it or of their mother laughing at their antics. Nor of I with her.

The pilot taxied the plane to its hangar and parked. Part of me wished I could tell him to turn it around and take me back to Italy. But would my pain be less there? Hadn't it come when I witnessed the happiness of my friend and his wife? Could I bear seeing it again?

I stood and stretched my legs, noticing from the window that my valet was pulling my Mercedes-Benz convertible out into the sun and lowering the top. The weather today was perfect, as it was most days this time of the year on the island.

I took a step down the plane's ramp and gripped the handrail when I was overcome by what felt like a hurricane-force gale. The air around me went still, like the calm before the storm, or had it already been? I rubbed my temple with my other hand as Celestina's voice spoke to me. *"Kensington is in danger. Go to her, Cortez. Hurry."*

I spun around, back into the plane. "File an emergency flight plan," I told the pilot. "I must get to London immediately."

31

Kensington

"Shall we try again to have lunch today?" Linc asked when our four-hour morning meeting broke up.

"Sounds good to me, if we have time."

He smiled at me the same way he had yesterday. "We have time."

Also like yesterday, I sent Teagon a text, informing her that I was headed out to lunch.

"What sounds good?" Linc asked as we exited the building.

"Um…anything is fine…" I checked my phone when I didn't get a response from Teagon. She always responded within seconds. I suppose she could be in the loo, but even then, she responded.

"Everything okay?"

I scratched my forehead, studying my phone and willing the three little dots to appear and ease my mind. When they didn't, I bit my lower lip. "I'm sorry to do this to you two days in a row, but I need to run home and check on something."

"Would you like me to go with you?"

Still no dots. What in the bloody hell?

"Kensington?"

"I'm sorry, what?"

"I asked if you wanted me to go with you?"

"No, no. It's fine, I'm sure. Go on and get lunch, and I'll meet you back at the office."

"You're certain?"

"Quite," I answered, still studying my phone.

"Can I get you a cab?"

"That would be great, thanks." The hair on the back of my neck stood up. Something was wrong; I could feel it. Maybe she'd slipped in the shower and hit her head. Or maybe it was as simple as she'd been called to a meeting at MI6 and couldn't answer her phone. That's probably all it was. But wouldn't she have sent a text, telling me so?

"Here you go," said Linc, holding the door of the cab open for me. "You're certain you don't want me to come along?" he asked again.

"No, but thanks so much. I'll see you later." I gave the driver my address, and as he sped away from the building, I realized I'd probably just made it really bloody hard for whomever was on my detail today to keep up with me. I turned around, but didn't see any cabs following directly behind. *"Fuck,"* I muttered under my breath.

When the driver pulled up to my grandparents' house—mine now, it was hard to remember that—I handed him a few pounds and raced to the front door. Chills went up and down my spine when I put my hand on the knob and it opened. I didn't hear the alarm beeping either. Something was very wrong.

"Teagon?" I called out. "Hello?" I was about to turn around and walk back out when a hand went over my mouth.

"Kenzie, *édesem,* I've been waiting for you."

I almost wretched, hearing Konstantine's voice.

"Where is Teagon?" I cried when he moved his hand.

"Your friend? She and I hadn't met, Kenzie. Why is that? Do you think I'm not good enough to meet your friends?"

"Where is she, Konstantine?" I tried to move my head, but he'd moved his hand to my throat, and his grip was too tight. "Tell me where she is, or—"

He gripped harder, cutting off my windpipe, just like he had that night in the hotel room.

"You've made things very, very difficult for me, Kenzie. You know this, yes?"

"I…" It was impossible to try to talk. I grabbed at his fingers, trying to loosen his hold on me. I was losing strength quickly, and soon I'd lose consciousness. I was beginning to see black spots and feeling dizzy when I heard a commotion at the front door.

"Konstantine, let her go!" I heard Rile yell.

Konstantine's grip loosened. Not enough for me to get away, but I could breathe. I cried out when he jammed something into my side.

"Come closer and I'll kill her. Don't think I won't." He turned so I was staring directly at Cortez. Konstantine moved his arm around my neck and tightened his grip. He shoved whatever was at my side in harder. "I know you. You're one of Otto's men," he shouted. "My fucking cousin won't give up. You tell him that she is *mine*. I'll kill her before I let him get his hands on her," he screeched.

"Didn't you hear? Otto married last week. He doesn't want Kensington."

I heard Konstantine's voice hitch at the same time I saw Cortez's eyes shift for a split second. Someone was behind us. Maybe Teagon?

"You're a liar!" shouted Konstantine. "You're try-ing to trick me."

"Kensington is all yours now. You don't want to hurt her. If you do, you'll lose everything. Your money, your family…Drop the gun, Konstantine. We both know you won't kill her."

"You work for Otto. I know you do. You'll soon be out of a job because I'm going to kill him too. It didn't work the first time, but I found someone better this time."

Cortez's eyes flared, and I could feel his rage. At the same time, he reminded me to stay calm. He'd protect me. He'd always protect me. Because he loved me.

I calmed my mind, forcing everything out but him. I slowed my frantic breathing so it matched his. Kept my eyes on his.

He took one step closer, and I groaned when Konstantine shoved what I knew was a gun, harder into my side. I blinked and then refocused. Could Cortez read Konstantine? I couldn't, but I wasn't meant to. I had to stay open only to Cortez, so if there was some-thing I needed to know, feel, do, I could.

"Don't come closer!" Konstantine shouted when Cortez took one more step.

"You couldn't do it, Konstantine. You wanted to, but you couldn't."

"I could have. You don't know anything!"

Cortez shook his head. "You couldn't. Somewhere deep inside you, you knew you couldn't kill. Not Otto, not Kensington."

"He doesn't have to, because I'm here. Don't worry, my sweet boy. I will kill her. Once she's gone, the madness will end," I heard a female's voice say. I tore my eyes from Cortez's and saw Konstantine's mother step inside the side door. She held a gun pointed at Cortez.

The tension in Konstantine's body eased as though a great weight had been lifted. "It won't stop, Mother. It'll never stop."

"It will, precious. Trust me. I know."

His hand trembled.

Kensington, stay with me.

My eyes snapped back to Cortez.

Breathe, my darling.

"*No!*" shouted Konstantine, as if he was in some kind of pain. "*No.*" This time, he groaned.

"*Konstantine!*" his mother shouted. "*Look at me!*"

"*No, Mother. It won't stop.*"

Cortez's eyes were no longer on mine. He was laser-focused on the man who had me trapped in his arms. The look on his face conveyed the rage I felt seeping off of him.

Konstantine's body jerked, and he let out a gut-wrenching cry.

"Now!" Cortez shouted.

I heard a loud crash. Konstantine's mother jerked the gun in the direction of the sound of footsteps running from the back of the house. Shots rang out, and she fell to the floor. At the same time, Konstantine shoved me from him. Another gun fired, he fell to the floor, and I raced into Cortez's arms.

"Teagon?" I tried to pull away from him, but he held me tight.

"Where's Angel?" he shouted to the men who were checking the two bodies lying on the floor.

"Here!" one of them answered from the kitchen.

I tried again to break free of him, but Cortez tightened his grip.

"What in the bloody hell?" I heard her groan and exhaled the breath I'd been holding.

"Hang on," the man with her said. "Let me look you over."

Cortez released me when we both heard her say, "Crash, I'm fine." I raced over and knelt down beside her.

"Not you too? Gawd. I'm bloody fine." She smiled, but then turned serious. "I'm so sorry, Kenz."

"Don't be. I'm the one who started this whole mess."

"Are they dead?"

Crash nodded. "They are."

I could feel Cortez standing behind me. "Come, let's get you both out of here. Angel, Crash will take you to the hospital to be checked over."

"Rile—"

I'd seen him level that particular gaze before, and evidently, Angel had too since she didn't argue further.

"What about you? Tell me how he hurt you." Cortez cupped my cheek with his palm.

"I'm fine," I said, repeating Teagon's words. "I thought you were in Italy?"

"I was."

I didn't know where to look, his gaze was so intense. "Kensington, we must talk."

"What else is wrong, Cortez? I don't think—"

32

Rile

I lifted her into my arms like I had the first night I'd whisked her out of Konstantine's clutches, and held her as close to me as I could.

"Cortez?"

"Soon, my darling, I promise."

I carried her outside to where Casper was waiting with the SUV. I wouldn't bother taking her to my flat. I needed to get her farther away from here.

Before I told Casper where to go, I turned to where Kensington sat beside me in the back seat. I cupped her cheek with my palm like I had a few minutes ago. "Will you come with me to Mallorca?"

"Now?"

"Yes, now, Kensington."

She studied me, her eyes boring into mine. She had so many questions, but she and I needed to figure out the answers together.

"Is this for my protection, Cortez?"

"No, my love. It is for us."
"Then, yes."

We didn't talk en route to the airfield nor did we once we were on the plane. As soon as we were able to, I led her to the stateroom and held her in my arms.

I pushed away the memory of the pain I'd felt earlier when I couldn't escape seeing her life without me in it. Now I knew that wasn't what I was envisioning at all. I was seeing our life play out like a movie. There was no heartbreak. I knew this story would have a happy ending because I'd already seen it. I wondered if she had too.

My Mercedes, the one my valet had pulled out of the hanger early this morning, was still parked outside. As soon as the steps were lowered, I led Kensington to it. Before I opened the passenger door, I put my arm around her waist and kissed her. I was about to speak, but she put her fingers on my lips.

"Wait until we're home, Cortez."

The sun was setting when the plane landed, so it was dark by the time we drove through the gates of the house.

"Someone lit the fireplace," Kensington murmured while we waited for the garage door to open.

"Marta," I said, so she knew. "She did it a few minutes ago, before she left for the evening."

"We'll be alone?"

"Yes, my darling."

We rode the lift up to the solarium and sat side-by-side on the outdoor sofa, watching the moonlight play on the waves crashing on the shore below us. It was a perfect night made more so because the woman I'd love until I took my last breath, sat beside me.

I turned to her, and she turned to me. "I hope you can find a way to forgive me for breaking your heart, Kensington. I was so wrong."

"You were so wrong, Cortez, and yes, I forgive you."

"So easy on me. I don't deserve it."

"It's because I love you."

I closed my eyes and brought her hand to my mouth, kissing her palm. "I love you, my darling."

"I've known that all along."

I raised my brow and smiled. "I thought you'd given up on me."

She turned her body and rested her head against my shoulder. "I almost did."

"What made you change your mind?"

"It was a dream I had. I saw us, Cortez. The day we married. When our children were born. I saw you, by my side, for the rest of our lives, and I knew it would happen."

"When did you have this dream?"

"Last night. Yesterday, too. I never nap, but I kept falling asleep. Whenever I closed my eyes, I saw more of our life together."

"Would you believe me if I told you I had the same dreams?"

"More than I'd believe you didn't."

"You said you saw me with you?"

"Not just you, our children too."

"How many children?"

She looked over her shoulder. "Four, Cortez. I've always known we'd have four."

"Will our oldest be a boy or a girl?"

"You know our firstborn is a boy, Cortez. We had the same dreams."

I smiled when she nuzzled into me.

"Not the same."

"No? What makes you say they were different?"

"You saw me in your dreams."

"You didn't see me?"

"I didn't see myself."

"But we were here."

I breathed in her scent, wrapped my arms around her, making sure I wasn't dreaming now. I kissed her cheek and down her neck. "I will be right back, my love. Will you wait for me?"

"I would've waited forever, Cortez. I'm so relieved you didn't make me."

I slowly ran my fingers down her arm until we no longer touched and hurried into the bedroom. In the corner, there was an old wooden chest that had belonged to my grandmother on my father's side—also a queen.

I pulled out a small wooden box and a smaller one from inside it. I put it in my pocket and went back out to where Kensington waited.

Rather than sitting beside her, I got down on one knee. She gasped and brought both of her hands to her mouth.

"Francesca Alexandra Kensington Whitby, will you marry me?"

"Oh, yes."

I opened the box and took out the ring that had been left to me by my grandmother. "No other has worn this ring since Queen Sofia." I took her hand and slid it on her finger. The platinum setting held five pear-shaped diamonds and eighteen brilliant-cut diamonds. It fit Kensington's finger as though it was made for her.

Tears fell from her eyes as she studied it. "It's exactly how it looked in my dream."

33

Kensington

Cortez and I made love all night and then slept past noon. It was the first time we'd been at the house all by ourselves, and I loved it.

"How long will Marta be away?" I asked when we rode the lift to the lower level in search of food.

"I'm not certain she will be coming back."

"Because of me?" I gasped.

"No, no," he answered, cupping my cheek. "She is ready to retire and spend more time with her sister and her sister's family."

"Oh." I tried not to pout as I looked longingly at the homemade pastries she left for us.

"It's one of the many things you and I need to talk about in the coming days."

"That sounds ominous." I reached out and snatched a crumble cake. Cortez took a bite of it. "Hey, that was mine."

"What's mine is yours, and what's yours is ours. Except not everything."

I sat down at the table and took a sip of the tea he set in front of me. "That sounds worse than ominous. We just got engaged last night, and we're going to talk about a prenuptial agreement this morning?"

"Let me rephrase. What's mine is ours. Some things that are yours, will remain yours alone."

"How is that fair?"

"Because some of those things were passed down from your family."

"The same is true for you."

"Not really. I bought this house as well as my flat in London."

"What about the plane?"

"It depends on which plane you're speaking of."

"The first plane."

"I bought that as well."

"The money came from your family, though."

He shook his head. "Some, but not the bulk of it."

"You made enough money from working at MI6 to afford two multi-million dollar homes and an airplane? Teagon said MI6 paid well, but I never dreamed it was that well. Which reminds me, have you heard anything about her condition? I'd really like to talk to her today if I could."

Cortez smiled. "MI6 does not pay quite that well. I made many good investments with the money I inherited from my grandparents. Angel is fine, and that has been confirmed by Crash. And finally, yes, you may talk with her whenever you'd like."

As much as I didn't want to talk about what had happened yesterday, there were things I needed to know.

"How did you know to come to my house?"

"Come," he said, pulling me away from the table. "Let's go back to the solarium."

"Wait," I said when he pressed the button for the lift.

"Good thinking," he said when I got on carrying a plateful of crumble cakes.

We sat by the pool, dangled our feet in the water, and I raised my face to the sun.

"I was on my way back from Italy when something told me I had to get to London as soon as possible."

"Something or someone?"

He smiled. "I was already in the air when I received a call from Smoke, alerting me that Konstantine had escaped the psychiatric facility."

"There's more to it, isn't there?"

"I'm going to have to get used to this."

"They say to marry a woman who reminds you of your mother."

The smile that had momentarily left his face, came back, only to leave again. "Siren sustained injuries serious enough she required surgery. She's stable now. Smoke is with her. He'll keep me updated."

"You knew Konstantine would come to London."

"Yes. I also had reason to believe his mother aided his escape."

"He was stark-raving mad, Cortez."

"As, I believe, was she."

"Why in the world did he set his sights on me. I hardly knew him?"

Cortez explained what he'd learned at a meeting that took place at Buckingham Palace and how I was, evidently, the only single woman of marrying age that would fulfill the von Habsburg's crazy family statute about who heirs could marry. I shuddered at the archaicness of it.

"What about Otto? You told Konstantine he was married."

"And he was. It seems the von Habsburgs are willing to look the other way when the young woman one of the heirs weds is worth billions."

"Thank goodness we don't have to worry about him beating my door down."

"You'll soon be off the marriage market, my darling."

"Soon? Do you have a date in mind, Cortez?"

"Goodness, no. Whatever you'd like to do, I will go along with happily."

"Even if we wed tomorrow?"

He smiled. "Will that be enough time for your family to arrive?"

"Family?" I gasped. "If you're referring to Kiki and my father, good God, no. All the more reason for a small, simple ceremony. Your family can come, though."

"Is there anyone else you'd like to have in attendance?"

"Well, Teagon, of course. And maybe that Casper woman."

Cortez laughed out loud. "You want someone at our wedding that you refer to in such a way?"

"She's not all bad."

"What about Lincoln Mulrooney?"

This time I laughed out loud. "And why would I invite Linc?"

"So he sees for himself that you are my wife."

"You have no reason to be jealous of Linc." I bit my lower lip. "I do have to ring him, though."

"What will you tell him?"

"Well, specifically, I will tell him what happened yesterday, although it will likely be all over the news."

Cortez shook his head. "There will be no mention of it in the media."

My eyes opened wide. "Seriously? You can cover something like that up?"

"Can you imagine the state of affairs if foreign countries weren't able to? It's a right mess enough as it is. But, yes, to answer your question, it will remain out of the news. The von Habsburgs will want it that way, perhaps even more than the prime minister. By way of the Queen, of course."

"In that case, I suppose I won't tell Linc what happened. I have to tell him something, though, considering I went off to lunch and haven't returned."

"He is aware. However, I do encourage you to contact him, like Teagon, whenever you'd like."

"Cortez?"

"Yes, my love?"

"Never mind."

He smiled and cupped my cheek. "You've made a life for yourself in London."

"Not a life, but I do enjoy my work at Whitby Press. And at the hospital. I've been volunteering, but I suppose you already knew that."

"I think we can figure out a way to divide our time between here and there. We can also reside primarily in London if that's what you'd prefer."

"You wouldn't mind me going off to work every day?"

"I will proudly and happily support whatever it is you would like to do, Kensington. I love you."

"What about you and your work?"

"To be honest, I am ready for, as they say, a desk job."

"What does that entail?"

"Letting the younger crowd get their hands dirty while I orchestrate from my solarium." He waved his hand in a sweeping motion over the pool. "To answer your question in a serious way, it doesn't matter where we live, my darling. As long as we are together, I can be at home anywhere."

Epilogue

Rile

We were married in the small chapel on our estate on Mallorca in October, exactly one year after I first held Kensington in my arms.

My family was in attendance, which included my parents, my brother and his family, and my uncle and aunt, the King and Queen of Spain.

Kensington's father was with us along with other members of her family, including the royal ones. She marveled at how I'd managed to get her great-aunt there without the fanfare usually afforded reigning monarchs. In the case of our wedding, I told her, there was no royalty with us, only loving aunts and uncles.

I'd asked her more than once about not inviting her mother, but after the one conversation Kensington had had with Kiki, I knew it would be a long time before that relationship would be reparable.

Every member of the Invincibles team was with us, including my partners, Decker, Edge, and Grinder, and their wives and families. Kensington insisted we also invite Casper, Ink, and Crash. And I insisted we invite Linc Mulrooney.

Quint and Darrow Alexander flew over from Texas, and Quint's father, Z, the man who had once been the chief over most of the Invincibles, came too.

He was very put out with me when he heard I'd made an offer to Angel to join our team, but as a wedding gift, promised not to rail at me about it today.

Tomorrow after our remaining guests departed, we were leaving to return to Fregate Island in the Seychelles, where we would stay until after my birthday in November. When we returned, both Kensington and I hoped we would be well on our way to starting our family.

We'd spent more time on Mallorca in the last couple of months than I'd originally anticipated. Decker flew over and set up offices for both Kensington and I to be able to work remotely. She even attended the Whitby weekly staff meetings via video conferencing.

"Cortez, may I have a word?" asked my second cousin once removed.

"Of course, Your Majesty."

"I want you to know that I couldn't be happier for you and my grandniece. You make a beautiful couple."

"Thank you, ma'am."

She put her hand on my arm. "However, if you keep her here, in Spain, and not in London where I can see the two of you regularly, I shall be very unhappy."

"I promise we will spend a great deal of time in London."

"Very well. You may thank me now, Cortez."

"Thank you again, Your Majesty."

"What are you thanking me for, exactly?"

"For joining us today and—"

My mother wrapped her arm in mine. "My cousin is suggesting you thank her for her brilliant match-making abilities."

The Queen winked. "I told you he'd find his way."

The next morning, before we left on our honeymoon, Kensington asked if we could take a walk together to the cemetery. She'd taken flowers from her bouquet that she laid on Celestina's grave.

"Thank you," she whispered, tracing the letters carved into the stone with her fingertips. "I'll love him forever."

"Goodbye, my love," I heard Celestina's voice for what I knew would be the last time.

Kensington closed her eyes and smiled. When she opened them and looked at me, I saw her tears.

"What is it, my darling?"

"She told me that you will love me forever too, and then she said goodbye."

We walked back to the house, hand in hand, laughing to ourselves when Kensington said that, like the Queen, Celestina also had brilliant match-making skills.

Keep reading for a sneak peek
at the next book
in the Invincibles Series—
SMOKED!

1

Smoke

I held my breath when the doctor came out the double doors with a grim look on his face.

"Siobhan Gallagher's family," the nurse with him called out. I stood and walked toward them.

"That's me."

"Your name?"

"Broderick Torcher."

The doctor cleared his throat. "The surgery was successful, and Miss Gallagher is in stable condition."

I let out the breath I'd been holding, sensing there was a "but" coming. Sure enough, his next sentence confirmed it.

"There was brain trauma associated with her injuries…"

I felt the bile rising in my throat.

"Miss Gallagher has suffered a series of small strokes. Her speech and some movement has been affected, as well as her memory."

"Give it to me straight, Doc. What do you mean by 'affected'?"

"As with any stroke, when the patient first regains consciousness, the symptoms are typically at their worst. Some regain full mental and physical capacity immediately. Others, it takes longer."

I took another deep breath, restraining myself from grabbing the man by the throat, putting his back to the wall, and insisting he answer my fucking question. Instead, I spoke slowly. "What…exactly…is…her…mental…and…physical condition?"

"Miss Gallagher is having trouble controlling movement on the left side of her body, but she does have function. We expect this to improve relatively quickly."

"What are you leaving out?"

"Miss Gallagher appears to have no long-term memory."

"How quickly do you anticipate that will improve?"

"It would be premature to give you any definitive answers."

I rubbed the back of my neck, wishing I could turn around, walk out of the hospital, and never look back.

"What is the nature of your relationship with Miss Gallagher?"

"Work colleagues."

The doctor raised his brow and looked at the nurse, who opened the folder she had in her hand and shuffled through the papers inside. She handed him a sheet containing the information I assumed he was looking for.

"You're listed as having her medical power of attorney."

"That's right." The reason why was none of his business.

"It's unlikely she'll remember you."

"Understood."

He studied me for a moment. "Do you have any other questions?"

I shook my head.

"You may see her now. If you'd like, the nurse can escort you to her room."

If I'd like? There's nothing I'd *like* less. However, this wasn't something I could walk away from. Siren wasn't someone I could walk away from either.

About the Author

USA Today and Amazon Top 15 Bestselling Author Heather Slade writes shamelessly sexy, edge-of-your seat romantic suspense.

She gave herself the gift of writing a book for her own birthday one year. Forty-plus books later (and counting), she's having the time of her life.

The women Slade writes are self-confident, strong, with wills of their own, and hearts as big as the Colorado sky. The men are sublimely sexy, seductive alphas who rise to the challenge of capturing the sweet soul of a woman whose heart they'll hold in the palm of their hand forever. Add in a couple of neck-snapping twists and turns, a page-turning mystery, and a swoon-worthy HEA, and you'll be holding one of her books in your hands.

She loves to hear from my readers. You can contact her at heather@heatherslade.com

To keep up with her latest news and releases, please visit her website at www.heatherslade.com to sign up for her newsletter.

MORE FROM AUTHOR HEATHER SLADE

BUTLER RANCH
Kade's Worth
Brodie's Promise
Maddox's Truce
Naughton's Secret
Mercer's Vow
Kade's Return
Butler Ranch Christmas

WICKED WINEMAKERS
FIRST LABEL
Brix's Bid
Ridge's Release
Press' Passion
Zin's Sins
Tryst's Temptation

WICKED WINEMAKERS
SECOND LABEL
Beau's Beloved
Coming Soon:
Cru's Crush
Bones' Bliss
Snapper's Seduction
Kick's Kiss

ROARING FORK RANCH
Coming Soon:
Roaring Fork Wrangler
Roaring Fork Roughstock
Roaring Fork Rockstar
Roaring Fork Rooker
Roaring Fork Bridger

THE ROYAL AGENTS
OF MI6
Make Me Shiver
Drive Me Wilder
Feel My Pinch
Chase My Shadow
Find My Angel

K19 SECURITY
SOLUTIONS TEAM ONE
Razor's Edge
Gunner's Redemption
Mistletoe's Magic
Mantis' Desire
Dutch's Salvation

K19 SECURITY
SOLUTIONS TEAM TWO
Striker's Choice
Monk's Fire
Halo's Oath
Tackle's Honor
Onyx's Awakening

K19 SHADOW OPERATIONS
TEAM ONE
Code Name: Ranger
Code Name: Diesel
Code Name: Wasp
Code Name: Cowboy
Code Name: Mayhem

K19 ALLIED INTELLIGENCE
TEAM ONE
Code Name: Ares
Code Name: Cayman
Code Name: Poseidon
Code Name: Zeppelin
Code Name: Magnet

K19 ALLIED INTELLIGENCE
TEAM TWO
Coming Soon:
Code Name: Puck
Code Name: Michelangelo
Code Name: Typhon
Code Name: Hornet
Code Name: Reaper

PROTECTORS
UNDERCOVER
Undercover Agent
Undercover Emissary
Coming Soon:
Undercover Savior
Undercover Infidel
Undercover Assassin

THE INVINCIBLES
TEAM ONE
Decked
Edged
Grinded
Riled
Smoked

THE INVINCIBLES
TEAM TWO
Bucked
Irished
Sainted
Hammered
Ripped

THE UNSTOPPABLES
TEAM ONE
Furied
Merried

COWBOYS OF
CRESTED BUTTE
A Cowboy Falls
A Cowboy's Dance
A Cowboy's Kiss
A Cowboy Stays
A Cowboy Wins

www.ingramcontent.com/pod-product-compliance
Lightning Source LLC
Chambersburg PA
CBHW070615300726
48975CB00006B/1818